THE RECKONING OF MEN

THE RECKONING OF MEN

THE RECKONING OF MEN

THE CROCKETTS' WESTERN SAGA
BOOK 13

ROBERT VAUGHAN
CHRIS MULLEN

WOLFPACK
PUBLISHING
— EST 2013 —

The Reckoning of Men
The Crocketts' Western Saga: Thirteen
Paperback Edition
Copyright © 2025 by Robert Vaughan and Chris Mullen

Wolfpack Publishing
1707 E. Diana Street
Tampa, FL 33610

wolfpackpublishing.com

Paperback ISBN 979-8-89567-214-3
Ebook ISBN 979-8-89567-213-6
LCCN 2025939099

THE RECKONING OF MEN

THE RECKONING OF MEN

CHAPTER ONE

"HOLY COW, GID! I KNEW'D YOU COULD EAT, BUT THIS here takes the cake!" Will laughed.

Will Crockett watched his big, little brother dive into a second blueberry pie face first, with hands clasped behind his back. Without coming up for air, and slurping like his life depended on it, Gid devoured the second pie before the other two contestants at the Clarendon, Texas, Main Street Fair pie-eating contest had even finished their first. The crowd cheered, then broke into rolling laughter when Gid sat up in his chair, his face a purple mess of blueberries and bits of pie crust.

"Well, folks," Bill Fitch, the mayor of Clarendon, announced. "It seems we have a new winner this year." Mayor Fitch approached the table with a large, hand-carved wooden fork and handed it to Gid. "By the power vested in me, I pronounce you..." He paused and leaned forward, whispering to Gid, "Tell me your name again."

"This here is Gid Crockett," Will proclaimed. "Biggest appetite in the territory."

"I'll agree to that," Gid replied, holding up the wooden fork in victory.

"Yes. Yes," Mayor Fitch agreed. "To accompany the coveted Wooden Fork trophy is an all-you-can-drink certificate at Blueberry Mike's Saloon and Eatery."

Gid looked at Will and smiled, showing his teeth speckled with blueberry skin.

"Come on, Gid," Will said, walking around behind the table. "Best git you cleaned up if you're gonna enjoy your winnings."

"Sounds good to me, Will." Gid turned to Mayor Fitch. "You plannin' on joining us, Mr. Mayor?"

"Well, boys, I don't mind if I do."

The other contestants, one of whom looked no older than thirteen, stood up and dispersed among the crowd, each marveling at how fast Gid had eaten his pies. The thirteen-year-old's shoulders hung low. Gid noticed as he, Will, and Mayor Fitch had started for Blueberry Mike's when he placed a hand on Will's shoulder.

"Y'all go on. I got somethin' I need to do first."

Will followed Gid's look, and when his eyes fell upon the boy, Will knew what Gid had up his sleeve.

"All right, Gid. See you inside. We'll make sure to save you a seat."

Will and Mayor Fitch ambled on to the boardwalk that paralleled Main Street and the buildings thereupon and disappeared into the crowd of fairgoers. Gid, remembering what it was like to be a little brother and always losing contests to Will, caught up with the boy. "Hey there, kiddo."

The boy turned around, his face was stained purple like Gid's, and his eyes were red and hazy with held-back tears.

"Come on now," Gid said. "Ya done good. No need for all that."

The boy wiped his nose on his sleeve.

"What's yer name?" Gid asked.

"Name's Henry, but most people call me Buster."

"Well, okay, Buster. I want you to have this." Gid pulled the wooden fork out of his pocket and handed it to the boy. "Kid like you, growin' big as ya are. Heck. Yer the real winner in my book."

Buster marveled at the prized fork.

"Go on," Gid said. "I want ya ta have it."

As Buster revered the prized fork, a loud voice boomed out from the side. "Ain't no sense in pityin' a loser. Ya gonna make 'im soft if'n ya give 'im that fer nuthin'."

Gid and Buster turned to see a medium-sized man in a dirt-stained, long-sleeved cotton shirt, trousers held up by one suspender, and boots that looked near ten years old.

"Go on, Henry. Give 'er back."

"But, Pa," Buster pleaded.

"Don't ya *Pa* me. Git yer butt back ta the wagon. We're headin' home."

"But the fair ain't over yet. We'll miss the fireworks if we leave now."

Buster's pa looked at Gid square in the eyes. Gid knew his kind, but there was little he could do or say to the man.

"Ya shoulda thought a that before losin' ta this big-bellied buffoon."

"Hold on, mister," Gid said. "There ain't no—"

"Name's Cletus Morgan, and I'll be the one ta say what is er what ain't. Hear me?" Cletus turned back to

Buster, whose eyes had turned red and filled with tears once again. "Do as I say or I'll tan yer hide, boy."

Buster turned for the wagon when Cletus stopped him. "Ain't ya forgettin' sumthin'?"

Upset and embarrassed, he looked at the prized fork in his hand, then held it out to Gid. "Here, mister."

Gid wanted Buster to keep the fork, but he did not want to cause him any more trouble.

"Thanks, Buster. You ever want a rematch, you let me know."

Buster nodded, then whirled around, ran down the street, and hopped into the bed of a wagon that had seen better days.

Cletus stood by Gid and watched his son's disappointment spill out on his sleeve.

"That make ya feel good, Mr. Morgan?"

"Don't care one way er the other. Ain't no boy a mine gonna think second fiddle's good enough." With that, Cletus stomped off to his wagon, loaded up, and continued to chastise Buster as they drove out of town.

———

A FEW MOMENTS LATER, Gid joined Will and Mayor Fitch at a table inside Blueberry Mike's.

"What took you so long, Little Brother?" Will asked. "You look like someone just stole yer favorite horse."

Gid grabbed the glass of beer Will had placed in front of him and downed it in three long, frothy gulps. "Everything's fine, Will. Just making a new friend is all."

"A new friend, huh? Well, if you ask me, I ain't never seen you so blue, and that ain't even because of all that pie still stuck on your face. Cheer up, Gid. Wipe your face and let's see if Mayor Fitch will introduce us to a couple of the gals over there."

Will pointed, and as things usually turned out, needed no introduction to meet and befriend two beautiful ladies waiting for a chance to make new friends of their own.

CHAPTER TWO

"SHE-OOT FIRE! I HEAR'D THERE'S A BIG TADO IN TOWN an' we ain't got hide nor hair betweens us fer funnin'."

"Would, 'cept ya blew what we had at the Faro tables in Tascosa. It's a wonder we got outta town without our necks bein' stretched or a bullet in our backs. Next time, I'll do the gamblin' so's we ain't gots ta steal ta survive. My butt's sore from ridin', an' my stomach's still growlin' on account of it bein' empty fer so long."

Tater and Sully McPherson sat around a dwindling campfire, grumbling about their self-inflicted bad luck and how they never had a chance at an easy life.

"I tell ya this," Sully said, holding his stomach. "I go much longer without a bite, I may just cut off yer leg an' throw it on the fire."

Tater looked at his brother, eyes widening, then split his face into a wide grin. "Well, if'n it comes ta that, save some fer me."

CHAPTER THREE

CLETUS MORGAN AND BUSTER HEADED FOR HOME, bouncing along the hard-packed trail in their rickety wagon. Buster had run out of tears but still felt bad about what happened between his pa and Gid back in town. It was not enough to lose the pie-eating contest and be shamed in front of everybody, but now he was missing the fireworks show as well. That was supposed to be the big event. And he had promised to meet Mary Sue near the water well to watch them together. Buster's whole day, and what seemed like his entire life, felt like it was crashing down around him.

"Quit yer mopin', Henry," Cletus said, noticing his son's disposition. "When I wuz yer age, ain't nobody give me nuthin'. Not my pa. Not Mother. Not any of my brothers er sisters. I had ta scrap fer everythin' jus' ta survive."

Buster looked at Cletus. "Nothing? Granny says ya always had food on the table, even when Paw-paw was away. She says everyone pitched in for the good of the family."

"Yer Granny is an old bag a bones who cain't remember a danged thing. Heck, she wouldn't remember yesterday if it slapped her in the face."

Cletus leaned forward and gave a sharp snap of the reins. The wagon groaned as the horses increased their gait. The limited supplies Cletus had procured in town —one bag of flour, one bag of beans, a new stock pot, a pouch of salt, three muslin wraps of salted beef, and a quarter barrel of seed—jostled in the bed of the wagon.

"Git back there an' make sure nuthin' breaks open er tumps over. Ain't much, but cain't afford ta lose what we got. Ya lose anythin', it'll be more than yer pride that aches, boy."

Buster scrambled over the bench seat and into the back of the wagon, stretching his limbs wide to brace their meager supplies.

Cletus snapped the reins again. The horses responded with an abruptness that caused Buster to lose his balance. With wide, horrified eyes, he watched the bag of beans he had been supporting slump and spill out over the wood decking. The rat-a-tat-tat scatter of beans sent an icy chill through his veins. Buster clenched his jaw, expecting his pa to turn around with a wicked scolding.

He did not turn around. He did not lash out. Instead, it seemed something ahead had caught his pa's eye.

"Smoke ahead," he said. "Ain't even near supper-time. Who the hell is burnin' a fire this time of day?"

CHAPTER FOUR

MAYOR FITCH SAT ACROSS FROM WILL AND GID, a sea of empty beer glasses between them. To Will's left sat Adriana, a feisty Latina wearing a pink silk rose in her hair. Gid held no company at present, not for lack of want, but more so due to a lack of trying. His thoughts were elsewhere, which made him difficult company to keep if you were a lady on the job.

"So, fellas, what brings you to Clarendon this time of year? If yer looking for work, I may know a spread or two who's hiring?"

"Thank you, Bill." Will paused to take a sip of beer from a fresh glass Adriana had set before him. He gave her a nod, acknowledging her attentiveness, and continued the conversation with the mayor. "It's just that, we ain't fer hire."

Mayor Fitch raised an eyebrow. His wonderment preceded his next statement. "You two look too well-kept to be drifters. Bounty hunters, perhaps?"

Gid leaned back in his chair and stretched his arms

above his head. "Bill, if ya ain't heard of us before today, that's a good thing fer us."

Mayor Fitch tilted his head, a perplexed look washing over him.

"What my brother means is that we have a pretty storied past, what with our experiences in the war and all our adventures since. We've been everywhere, dodgin' bullets, bringing men to justice, sendin' some to the grave."

Mayor Fitch dry-gulped.

"No need to worry, Bill," Will continued. "We're the good guys. We own the Brown Spur near Saginaw, round-a-bouts Fort Worth, but turns out ranchin' ain't in our blood. It's the unknown that calls to us."

"I'll drink to that," Adriana exclaimed, hoping to draw Will's attention back to her.

The men's gaze fell on her, but the moment was short-lived when two burly men walked into Blueberry Mike's with raised shotguns and ill intent on their minds.

The first man was large in the middle with gnarled brown teeth that showed when he smiled. A week's worth of stubble poked from his weathered face. His ugliness extended to his actions. Growling at a table nearest him, he aimed the shotgun above his head and pulled the trigger, blowing a hole in the ceiling.

The second man, skinny from his shins to his neck, wore a dark brown bowler with a tear in the brim. His cheeks stuck out like bony dams beneath his beady eyes. He sneered, waving a short-barrel shotgun in front of him, and spoke with a raspy, high-pitched tone. "Only movin' anyone needs be doin' is throwin' their hands in the air an' tossin' what they got in my man's hat when he comes by ta collect. Think yer fast enough, try us an' let ever' one sees ya get blow'd in two."

The crowd in Blueberry Mike's fell quiet. Will squeezed Adriana's thigh, signaling her to get ready to move aside. Mayor Fitch trembled.

The armed bandits went to work, one collecting valuables, the other threatening to shoot anyone who moved.

"I'll handle this," Gid said below his breath. What had been an enjoyable day had turned sour as of late, and he had more than enough if it.

"What er you doin', Gid?" Will whispered from the corner of his mouth.

"Nothin' that wouldn't surprise ya, big brother."

Gid waited until the bandits turned their backs, then slid his chair back and stood. A woman at a neighboring table shrieked when she saw him move, drawing the attention of the armed men and ruining his surprise.

"What the hell er ya doin'?" the man in the dingy bowler hat said.

The larger man placed his hat, heavy with stolen money and valuables, on the nearest table and raised his shotgun to point it at Gid. "Yeah, ya wants ta git sawed in two?"

Gid showed his hands were empty but, to the crowd's astonishment, continued to move toward the men. "Look, fellas. Ya mind if I get a refill? I just ate what feels like a pound of blueberry pie, and I could really use another beer to help wash it down."

The large man grinned, watching Gid inch his way closer.

"Ya sure are some kind of stupid," the larger man

said. Letting the end of his barrel sag, he turned to his partner. "Hear that, Jed? This fella says he's thirsty."

Will slowly twisted in his chair, careful not to let Adriana slip from his lap. His fingers inched toward the grip of his pistol. To his advantage, Adriana's legs, barely covered by her scanty chemise, concealed his movements, though she felt a sudden thrill when his bare knuckles brushed against the outside of her thigh.

"I done told ya not ta use our names!" Jed looked dumbfounded. He turned toward Gid and pointed the barrel of his shotgun at his midsection. "Cain't drink nuthin' if'n ya ain't got a gut."

Gid locked eyes with Jed. His pupils flickered, which was just what Gid had hoped to see. He took another step. The crowd looked on.

One man near the back of the saloon called out in a low, concerned voice, "Sit down, friend. He's gonna shoot ya."

Will slid his pistol from his holster. Adriana's mouth curled as the steel shaft pressed against her hip.

"Better listen ta that man over there, mister," the larger man said.

Gid stopped, now just two arm-lengths from the muzzle of Jed's shotgun, and raised a questioning eyebrow.

"What man?" He sounded baffled.

Jed huffed. Gid watched. Will waited. The large man's belly jiggled as he laughed at Gid's foolishness.

"Hell," Jed said. "Ya ain't only stupid, but deaf too? It was that man right back there."

It only took a moment for Jed to break eye contact and motion with his shotgun to the man in the back of the room for Gid to move.

With one quick burst of speed, Gid lunged forward, his hand locking onto the shotgun's barrel. In a single, forceful motion, he yanked it upward as Jed pulled the trigger, sending the shot wide and blasting a second hole in the ceiling. The sharp scent of burnt gunpowder filled the air as splinters and dust rained down on the saloon floor. A woman at the bar screamed.

The large man aimed his shotgun at Gid, but Will drew his pistol faster and shot him once in the belly and a second time in the hand. He dropped the shotgun and fell to the floor, grabbing his stomach and kicking out his legs from the pain.

Gid wrestled with Jed, his grip tightening on the barrel, his fingers burning from the heat, but he did not let go. Using the gun as leverage, Gid pulled back, lifting Jed off the ground, then propelled his own body forward. The sudden jerk and surge helped Gid ram the shotgun barrel into Jed's face, breaking his nose with a hair-raising crack. Dazed and in bloody pain, Jed staggered backward. Gid swiped the shotgun away from him, then recoiled and hit him across the face with the stock of the gun. Jed collapsed in a messy, unconscious heap. Blood from his cheek and broken nose painted a fresh stain on the dusty, wooden floor.

A roar erupted from inside the saloon, then died as quickly as it arose when the sheriff and two deputies burst through the batwing doors. With guns raised and eyes seeking out trouble, the sheriff spotted Will with his pistol drawn and Gid standing over Jed, holding the shotgun.

"Drop 'em!" he ordered.

A murmur swept through the crowd. Now that the danger had passed, Mayor Fitch straightened his coat and cleared his throat. Upon regaining his composure, he stood behind the table that he shared with the brothers.

"Put down your weapons, Sheriff Wolfe. The fight's over. See for yourself." He walked around the table and joined Will at his side. "These men are heroes."

The sheriff's deputies lowered their guns, but Sheriff Wolfe was not so quick to act.

"This is Will Crockett," Mayor Fitch continued. "That's his brother Gid. These men singlehandedly subdued these scoundrels, saving this fine establishment from absolute calamity."

Sheriff Wolfe holstered his pistol. "I'm Ed Wolfe. Sounds like we're in yer debt." He held his hand out to Will.

"The first shake should go to my brother, Gid. He's the one who saved the day."

The sheriff turned and stepped over to Gid. "Mighty brave of ya ta put yerself in harm's way."

"Just needed something to wash down some pie, and these two got in my way," Gid said as they shook.

"That so?"

"Something like that, anyways."

Sheriff Wolfe thanked Will, then shook the mayor's hand out of respect for his office, though he knew how cowardly Bill Fitch could act at times. Turning to his deputies, he waved them over.

"Grab a few able-bodied men an' drag these two outta here. Send someone fer Doc Bray. Have 'im meet ya at the jail. The skinny one looks fine. The fat one needs tendin' to."

As the sheriff and his deputies dragged the bandits away, the patrons of Blueberry Mike's began to breathe again. Will and Gid sat back down at their table. Adriana quickly returned to her spot on Will's lap, her hand squeezing his leg as she sat down. Mayor Fitch ordered fresh beers for all and Blueberry Mike himself delivered a fresh pie for the brothers to enjoy.

"It's on the house, gentlemen!"

Looking at the pie, Gid rubbed his belly, letting out a small groan. "Not sure I could eat another bite," he said, puffing out his cheeks.

Will cocked his head, his lips curling into a bemused smile. "Gid, I never thought I'd see the day when you'd turn down fresh blueberry pie!"

CHAPTER FIVE

CLETUS SQUINTED AS HE SURVEYED THE TRAIL AHEAD, HIS eyes locking on two men he saw huddling around a smoldering fire. One knelt, poking a stick into the dying coals. The other man stood behind him, pointing as if giving instructions.

"Hmmm," Cletus's throat rumbled.

He eased up on the reins. Their slowing speed made Buster worry that his failure to keep the supplies from spilling would soon earn him a sharp punishment.

"I'm sorry, Pa. I tried to..."

"Shut yer mouth, boy."

When Cletus did not turn around, Buster leaned out of the wagon bed and looked ahead.

"What is it, Pa?"

"You stay down, Henry."

"Pa? What do ya..."

"Do what yer told, an' keep quiet!"

Confused, yet relieved that he was not the focus of his pa's irritation, Buster hunkered down in the wagon bed, quietly scooping up loose beans and slipping them into his pockets, saving as many as he could before they rattled through the slates in the wagon and were lost for good.

The wagon bounced over the earth, hitting what felt to Buster like every large stone in their path. Each thud was jarring, each bounce the birth of a fresh bruise on his backside.

A thin line of smoke wafted into the sky. Cletus watched as the kneeling man stood up and kicked at the dead fire. Ash flew in the air in a puff of gray and white. Hiding in the rear of the wagon, Buster heard men begin to argue, then saw his pa's hand reach around the driver's bench, his fingers feeling for the stock of his Remington Model 1873 Hammer Lifter.

"I TOL' ya it ain't gonna catch. Ya done smothered it out!" Tater griped.

"Well, If'n ya hadn't put them green branches o'er the top, maybe it woulda kept burnin'. Yer the one who kilt the flame." Sully knocked his right boot heel on the ground, then stomped to get the leftover ash off the scuffed leather.

Tater stepped close to Sully, poking his chin out and sneering.

Sully puffed out his chest, bumping Tater.

The two brothers were at their wits' end. They were hungry, out of money, and now, even the fire was too much for them to manage. With no good sense between them, there was only one thing left to do. Fight.

"Bump me again an' see what happens," Tater scoffed.

"Don't think I won't."

Sully barreled forward like a charging bull, leading with his chest. Tater stepped out of the way and raised his knee, catching his brother in the gut. Sully doubled over.

"That'll teach ya," Tater chided.

Sully took a deep breath and whirled around, cracking Tater across the mouth with the back of his hand. Tater shook his head, then lunged at Sully, who, this time, was ready and waiting.

Both brothers had been in plenty of fights, but neither had a winning record to show for their efforts. Sully grabbed Tater's neck. Tater wrapped his right arm around Sully's head. Locked together, the two lost their balance and fell to the ground. They rolled and rolled, grunting and cursing, neither aware that they had an audience approaching the edge of their camp.

Cletus tightened his grip on the reins, pulling the wagon to a stop. A sly grin crossed his face as he watched the brothers wrestle. "You two look like a couple fool chickens fightin' over a roost."

The strange voice was loud and just as abrasive. Its harshness caught the brothers' attention. Still holding each other, they stopped rolling and looked up to see a man in a one-horse wagon looking down on them from his driver's seat.

"Who the hell is that?" Tater wheezed, catching his breath

"How should I know?" Sully replied.

Tater looked up at the stranger, his nose wrinkled and one eye pinched closed. "Who you, an' who ya callin' fools, mister?"

"I'm Cletus Morgan, an' you two are the gall darn-dest fools I ever did see."

Sully and Tater let go of one another and scrambled to their feet just in time to see the business end of a double-barrel shotgun aimed right at them.

"Hey, mister," Tater said, raising his arms. "Ya mind pointin' that thing somewhere's else?"

"I'll point it where I point it." Cletus sneered, his voice sounding as thick as gravel in a barrel.

Sully nudged his brother with an elbow. "Sure is onery, ain't he."

Cletus spat.

"Ya plannin' on jus' settin' there all day, er kin we be gittin' on?" Tater complained.

"Yeah," Sully added. "We're headin' ta town ta watch the show. Don't wanna be late."

Buster had been told to stay down and out of sight, but the mention of the show in town meant only one thing—fireworks. Shuffling his feet over a scattering of loose beans, he tried to rise and look out but but his pa's hand shoved his head back down before he could.

"What'cha got in there?" Sully asked, stepping closer to the wagon.

Cletus scowled, then turned his head to chastise Buster. The moment he looked away, Sully grabbed the shotgun and yanked hard, pulling Cletus off the driver's bench. Tater joined in and helped overpower Cletus, shoving him to the ground while Sully wrestled the shotgun free. The horse bucked once, bolting a few steps before settling, the jostled wagon creaking behind it.

"Well, lookie here. If the tables ain't turned ol' timer," Sully said, pulling the hammer back on the chambered barrel. "Why don't ya stand up an' fetch our supplies."

Tater leaned close to Sully and whispered in his ear. "What supplies, Sully? We ain't got a lick."

"Them supplies," Sully replied, lifting his chin. "The ones in that there wagon. I figures he owes us that much fer stickin' this shotgun in both our faces."

Tater looked at the wagon. When he turned back to his brother, his face split into a knowing grin. "Oh, yeah. Them supplies er ours now. Sounds 'bout right ta me."

Cletus rose, brushed dirt from his shirt, and stomped once. "They ain't fer either of ya."

Sully pressed the barrel of the shotgun against Cletus's chest.

"You ain't gonna shoot me." Cletus spat again, this time hitting Sully's left boot with a string of brown slobber. "Ain't got the balls ta do it."

Sully looked at the mess on his foot and popped the shotgun's iron barrel into Cletus's chin. The knock split the skin, which immediately bled onto his shirt and trousers.

"Ya son of a..." Cletus started to say, lunging at Sully.

His movements were quick, causing Sully to flinch and pull the trigger. The shotgun erupted in a spray of pellets that penetrated Cletus's chest, throwing him backward. He collapsed like a forgotten rag doll and was dead before he hit the dirt. His chest was ruined. Blood soaked into the shredded cloth that remained around the hole in Cletus's torso, the rest of which began to form a growing red puddle beneath him.

The sudden blast also spooked the horse. It took off at a gallop with Buster still hiding in the wagon bed, turning for the trail that led back to town.

"What did you do?" Tater yelled, standing over Cletus.

Smoke curled from the barrel. The hot sting of gunpowder hung in the air.

"I dunno. I dunno!" Sully's mouth was agape, his gaze frozen at Cletus on the ground, whose eyes looked back at him, forever wide and staring in disbelief. "I weren't gonna shoot 'im. I didn't mean ta kill 'im!"

In a panic, Tater stomped. Sully's feet felt like lead. He dropped the shotgun and rubbed his cheeks over and over, unable to look away from what he had done.

"I ain't never kill't nobody." The lingering echo of the sudden blast rang in Sully's ears. "We gonna hang fer sure."

CHAPTER SIX

THE MAIN STREET FAIR BUSTLED WITH EXCITEMENT AS people gathered near the church square for the highly anticipated fireworks display. Fredrick Bumgartner and Hank Tillman stood by the hand pump engine, ready to ring the bell and summon the rest of the fire brigade should the show take a turn for the worse. Mary Sue waited near the water well for Buster. She hid two peppermint-flavored candy sticks behind her back to surprise him.

Little Davy Johnson ran up and down Main Street, ducking into the barber, the bank, the sheriff's office, and any building with an open door shouting at the top of his lungs. "Fireworks! Fireworks! Don't miss the show!"

His cadence was memorable, his enthusiasm enviable.

When Davy barged into Blueberry Mike's and made his announcement, Mayor Fitch slid his chair back and stood. "Will, Gid, would you accompany me to the bandstand as my special guests?"

Will polished off the last of his beer and wiped his mouth. "Don't see why not. Gid?"

Gid felt better with a few libations in him, but part of him still wished he had decked Buster's crotchety father in the mouth earlier. It would not have done any good and may have made life harder on Buster, but it would have been satisfying for sure. "All right, Will. Long as none of them skyrockets shoot at me."

"It's settled then," Mayor Fitch said.

Will and Gid followed him out of Blueberry Mike's through the bat wing doors and into the cool of the early evening. The horizon looked two shades of purple set beneath a roaring blaze of fiery oranges and yellows as if J.M.W. Turner had blurred the end of day and the coming night with the softest of brush strokes across the sky.

Mayor Fitch walked with a bounce in his step, his hands gripping the lapels of his jacket. "Look at all these fine people," he declared. "No better place around."

Will and Gid shared a look.

"Guess he's already forgotten about what just happened?" Gid muttered.

As they headed for a small bandstand erected in front of the church, a murmur rose from the gathered crowd. It started low, then became more pronounced when men began shouting.

"Look out!"

"It's a runaway!"

"Somebody, stop that wagon!"

Like a flock of birds evading a predator, the crowd split into two groups, swarming the boardwalk on one side of the street and the church entryway and bandstand on the other. The rattle and clank of an old wagon and the pounding hooves of a horse on the run grew louder beyond the calls for someone to intervene.

Mayor Fitch hurried to the boardwalk, bumping into the crowd to make room for himself. Will and Gid stood in the middle of the street, watching a driverless wagon barrel straight toward them.

"She's comin' on fast, Gid."

Gid squinted, sizing up the wagon. As the last rays of sunlight slipped beneath the horizon, a soft afterglow radiated across the sky, making the wagon harder to see as it stampeded closer. "Here goes nothin'," Gid said.

Before Will could react, Gid sprinted ahead, charging toward the wagon. Each pound of his boots seemed to draw in line with the rhythm of the horse's hooves.

As the horse and wagon passed between the group of onlookers, one man ran beside and tried to climb aboard. He grabbed the bed rail but lost his footing as he attempted to pull himself into the back of the wagon. He tumbled to the ground, the rear wheel missing his head by mere inches.

Gid did not let up. He continued to run straight for the wagon. The gap between them was closing fast.

"Careful, Gid!" Will called from behind.

A murmur rose through the crowd. At the last possible moment, Gid locked eyes with the horse, clenched his teeth, and with one powerful grab and lunge, sidestepped the stampeding animal, seized the harness around the horse's face, and used his forward momentum to leap and swing onto its bare back.

A roar erupted from the crowd, but Will continued to watch with intensity. Gid was not out of the woods yet.

Fighting for balance, Gid squeezed his legs around the horse's ribs and repositioned his hands to grip its mane. On they sped, passing Will and heading for the opposite end of town.

"C'mon, now. Take it easy," Gid said, his voice firm yet calming.

He pulled at the horse's head as if he held reins. The horse responded, slowing from an all-out run to a hard gallop and, finally, a labored trot. It snorted as its powerful strides lost their wild momentum.

Gid patted its neck as they came to a complete stop, then leaned forward and whispered into its twitching ears. "At-a girl. Ya done gave me a wild ride. What spooked ya so?"

A soft thud and rattle sounded out in the bed of the wagon as if small stones had just scattered across a wooden floor. Gid paid little attention until the soft sniffs of a frightened child rose from its berth as well.

Gid slid off the horse and walked back to the bed of the wagon, making sure to set the driver's brake in case the horse got a second wind.

"Someone back there?" Gid said. "Yer safe now. Why don't ya come on out."

Pounding feet slowed behind Gid as Will finally caught up. "Pretty ballsy, brother. You all right?"

"I'm fine, but I think there's someone in the back."

Will joined Gid by his side. "How you figure?"

No sooner had Will pondered Gid's comment than a small figure stirred among the toppled supplies. Debris fell away from Buster as he rose in the wagon bed. His hair was ruffled and covered with flour, some of which had caked onto his face and turned to white mud beneath his frightened tears.

"Buster?" Gid said, pulling himself onto the wagon's side rail. "That you?"

Buster's lips quivered, but he nodded.

"What the heck happened? Where is yer pa?"

"We...I...he..."

"Settle down, son," Will added. "Everythin's okay now."

"No," Buster said. "It ain't. I think..." Buster wiped his nose on his sleeve. "I think someone shot him. I think he's dead."

CHAPTER SEVEN

GID DROVE WILL AND BUSTER BACK TO THE CENTER OF town and parked the wagon alongside the sheriff's office. Sheriff Wolfe stood in the doorway, his eyes keen on the crowd gathered near the church for the fireworks show. Gid hopped off the driver's bench.

"With what I heard about ya overcomin' those men at Mike's, I figured ya fer a loose cannon. Now, seein' ya mount that horse at full speed and stop that runaway wagon, I'm sure of it." Sheriff Wolfe stepped forward and offered Gid a hand for the second time in so many meetings. He looked up at Will and Buster. "Looks like ya have everythin' under control. Nobody hurt, is they?"

Will glanced at Buster. "He ain't hurt, but he's sayin' his pa's been shot. Maybe killed."

"Cletus Morgan?" The sheriff lowered his voice, speaking to himself and shaking his head. "Man had a temper as short as them fuses about ta light them fire-crackers." He stepped past Gid and approached the side rail of the wagon. "You okay, son? Wanna tell me what happened?"

Buster's eyes were red, his cheeks tear-streaked and flushed. "I didn't see much," he started. "Pa made me stay down in the back on account of we was comin' up on someone's campfire. He had his shotgun ready, just in case, but when we stopped near the camp, Pa started talkin' like he does an' the two men there took it away. I peeked once. Pa was still standin' an' talkin' with the men. They said they wanted our stuff. Next thing, I hear a blast an' the horse takes off runnin' with me still in the back. I tried ta see Pa. Tried callin' out, but with every-thing bouncing around in the wagon, I couldn't get my balance and I was just...scared. All's I could see before the wagon topped the hill were my pa lyin' on the ground an' the two men yellin' at each other."

Sheriff Wolfe turned back to Gid. "You drive this wagon back to the Morgan place with Buster?"

"I can do that."

Will hopped down from the wagon. "I'll follow along with the horses, Gid."

Gid nodded at Will.

"Good. I'll ride with ya as far as the camp," Wolfe said. "See what, if anythin' to his story checks out."

Gid tipped his hat back. "Ya don't think he's makin' this up, do ya?"

"Part of me hopes he is. The other part tells me I've got a problem on my hands. An' the timing couldn't be worse. With all this show goin' on in town, we're likely ta experience a lively night around here."

Will looked at the crowd coming back together in the street before the church once again. Their chatter swept down Main Street like a cloud of cicadas moving across the town.

"We better get moving while there's still a little light left ta see."

Gid climbed back onto the driver's bench and took the reins. He heard Buster shuffling around in the wagon bed. Turning around, he patted the seat next to him. "Get on up here with me, Buster. No sense riding back there now."

Buster hesitated. The freight box was his usual spot coming and going to town. He never understood why he was not allowed to sit up front before, but now when the offer was presented to him, it did not feel right. "I'm suppos'd ta sit in the back. Watchin' the supplies is my job."

Sheriff Wolfe spoke up. "Henry Morgan, yer job tonight is ta lead us back ta that camp. There ain't no doin' that from the back. Climb on over an' let's go find yer pa."

"Yessir," Buster replied.

"Gid. Will. We run inta trouble out there, me and my depuites'll handle it. Ya done good at Blueberry Mike's, but I'm gonna need ya ta stay back unless I call on ya."

Will and Gid shared a look.

"We can handle ourselves," Will said.

"I ain't sayin' ya can't. Truth be told, I've heard yer names in the past. Didn't recollect 'em before, but they came to me just the same. I need ya ta remember that this is my town. I'm in charge an' will see that things are done proper."

"We're not lookin' for a fight, Sheriff. Will an' I help where help is needed. No more. No less."

Sheriff Wolfe nodded, then turned and walked into the sheriff's office. A moment later, he returned with two deputies, each armed with a Winchester Model 1873 and Colt pistols holstered on their hips.

"This is Charlie Withers an' Pierce McGraw," Sheriff Wolfe said. "Charlie's been with me the longest. Prob'ly stickin' around fer my job one of these days. Pierce came on near about six months ago. Both are capable, but moreover, I trust 'em."

Will, Gid, and the deputies regarded one another with a nod.

"Y'all head on," Sheriff Wolfe said. "We'll saddle up an' meet ya on the trail."

"And if we meet up with these men Buster was tellin' us about first?" Will asked.

"Don't see that happenin'. Those boys are long gone by now."

Sheriff Wolfe and his deputies headed out, disappearing into the alley beside the sheriff's office. Gid glanced at Will, then turned his gaze to Buster, now sitting next to him on the bench. "Don't you worry. Ain't nuthin' gonna happen to ya long as I have anythin' ta say about it."

Buster's eyes looked dark and deep in the advancing twilight, frightened by the runaway wagon and concerned about what they might find ahead. Gid knew the look. He had felt the same before. Thoughts of his parents flashed in his mind, transporting him back to that afternoon at the Crockett farm in Missouri when he and Will found their father murdered and their mother stripped naked and left for dead in the field. It had been over twenty years, but the images were clear as if he and Will had only just found them.

"I'll grab the horses," Will said. "We can tie yours to the back of the wagon, Gid."

Gid nodded, then released the hand brake and gave a gentle flick of the reins. "Walk on," he called. The wagon jolted as the horse began to pull them away from the sheriff's office.

Will headed for the stables at the far end of town to retrieve their horses.

As the wagon rolled past the crowd waiting for the fireworks show to begin, onlookers gave Gid and Buster odd looks. Gid ignored them. Buster did not notice. He had found the sorrow-filled gaze of Mary Sue watching him as they drove past the water well where she waited. Her hands were pressed together under her chin. Two peppermint candy sticks lay at her feet in the dirt.

CHAPTER EIGHT

ORANGE COALS GLOWED BENEATH AN UNATTENDED FIRE. A chorus of crickets playing fiddle set the tone of early evening while a swarm of gnats congregated over the cooling body of Cletus Morgan. The thudding of hooves grew distant as Tater and Sully ran their horses west. If not for the blanket of stars stretching overhead and night swallowing them whole, the horizon would have been nothing but a blur as they fled. Such was their fate in that moment—no plan, no destination, only the need to put miles between them and the biggest mistake of their lives. Sully and Tater ran, but regret was not the only thing chasing them.

CHAPTER NINE

THE TRAIL GREW DARK, BUT EVEN AT NIGHT, BUSTER knew the way. It was the same every time he and his pa went to town. Most times he would lay back in the wagon's bed and watch the stars pop into view. He would lace his hands and cradle his head and imagine what it would be like if he could reach out and pluck one from the sky. If he was quiet enough, he could hear the breeze rustle through the trees, bending branches and upending leaves above the rattle and clank of the wagon.

Now, Buster sat up front, leading the way to a place he wished he did not have to go. He watched the trail ahead, ignoring the starry sky, hoping he was wrong about the whole thing. More than once, Buster looked over his shoulder and wondered what the fireworks had looked like. The torture of it all was he could hear the distant report of each rocket exploding, but that was it. No color. No wonder. Just a far-off boom barely above the squeaks and groans of an old wagon and the occasional snort from the horse that pulled them along.

Sitting next to Gid, he was no longer scared by what happened, but grew more worried about what his life would look like come morning. Would he be made to blame? His family had already lost an older brother to fever last year. Devastated, his mother had not accepted his death, carrying the pain and guilt in her every look. How would she react this time? And his two younger sisters? It was all too much to digest at once that it made him feel sick to his stomach. Slouching on the bench next to Gid, Buster held his hands over his middle and tried not to think about anything else except how next year, no matter what, he would sit and watch those fireworks with Mary Sue.

———

SHERIFF WOLFE and his deputies had caught up as expected and rode alongside Will twenty feet behind the wagon. The moon had begun to rise over the trees to the southeast, casting a dull, white ambiance over the small posse and the trail on which they traveled.

"Sheriff, you said back in town that the men who killed Cletus would be long gone by now. Which direction do you think they headed?" Will asked.

"Depends. Lots of country out there. Ya got the wide-open plains to the north. Don't have ta worry much 'bout the Commanche anymore. Maybe a rogue band er two. Most were pushed ta reservations in Oklahoma.

"Ta the south ya got ranchlands. Plenty a work if ya can find a crew. Perfect fer blendin' in, especially if yer a hard worker. Then there's west."

Sheriff Wolfe paused and spat. "I'd only go that way

if I had plenty of supplies and weren't in a hurry. Ride too hard, too fast, and yer liable to run right off the Caprock Escarpment. Buzzards'll find ya before anyone else. Plus, with all them damn prairie dog towns, ya gotta watch the ground real careful—one wrong step and yer horse's legs'll break right off in a burrow. No, if I were them and had just killed somebody, I'm headin' south for sure. If ranchin' don't work out, Mexico ain't too far off ta let things cool down before headin' back across the river."

"I'm guessing if we find Cletus dead after all, you'll be puttin' together a group to find these men? You can count us in."

Sheriff Wolfe spat again. "Appreciate yer willingness, Will. I'll make that call once we get to the camp and find the body."

"Ya think the old guy is worth the fuss, Sheriff?" Deputy McGraw said. "I always figured he had it comin', what with the way he treated near everyone he came across."

Will turned his head to McGraw. "Every man, no matter how they run their life, deserves the benefit of the law. Dislike the man all you want. That doesn't mean he's afforded any less rights, whether he's alive or dead."

"Mr. Crockett. Seein' as you an' yer brother just got to town," Deputy Withers said. "Maybe it's best ta keep yer assumptions to yerself. Ya didn't even know the man."

Will pulled the reins left, slowing his horse and blocking the path of Deputy Withers. "Withers, right? Sure, I didn't know Cletus Morgan, but justice is the price a man pays for breakin' the law. Last time I checked, getting killed doesn't mean he's lost that right."

Sheriff Wolfe and Deputy McGraw stopped two horse lengths ahead of Will and Deputy Withers.

"Ya have a lot ta say about the law, Will. Seems as I recall the stories I've heard, you've had yer fair share on the other side," Sheriff Wolfe said. "I told ya I remembered yer name. Don't forget that."

"Sheriff, that was a long time ago." Will reined his horse out of Deputy Withers's path and walked over to a waiting Sheriff Wolfe and Deputy McGraw. McGraw chewed on the inside of his left cheek and glared at Will. "The Crockett name has been long since cleared. If you heard the stories, you knew that, too."

The wagon clanked ahead of them, drawing further away with each passing second.

"A-yuh," Sheriff Wolfe said. "I reckon I did."

Without another word, Will reined away and trotted ahead to catch up to Gid and Buster.

"Hey, Will," Gid said as his brother pulled alongside the wagon.

"How's Buster holding up?"

The brothers looked at the young boy, rocking in rhythm to the bumps and jolts of the trail. He stared ahead, still clutching his stomach.

"He sick or something?" Will asked.

"Just has a lot on his mind, I guess. Ain't said more than two words since we left." Gid flicked the reins. "What'd ya hear from the sheriff?"

"I'm hearin' plenty. It's what they're not sayin' that's startin' to get under my skin." Will's tone carried a hint of skepticism.

Gid shot Will a moonlit glance, his left eyebrow arching with curiosity.

"We may be headin' out to see if Cletus really is dead or if Buster was mistaken," Will continued. "But I think that's all that we're doin'. I'd bet my boots Sheriff Wolfe is aimin' to sweep this under the rug."

Gid grunted and glanced back at the trailing lawmen. Before he turned around, Buster sprang up from his seat and pointed ahead. "Just up there. Over that ridge." Buster's eyes widened with anticipation.

Gid faced the front and followed Buster's gaze. A chill crept up his spine as the image of his own father, lying shot dead on the farm, flashed through his mind.

"That's where they blasted Pa."

CHAPTER TEN

SULLY AND TATER DISMOUNTED BEFORE TRAVERSING McCullum Creek and stood on the banks of the once withered brook, now surging with angrier waters from a recent deluge to the north. If any luck was on their side at all, it came in the mindfulness of their horses to pull up before stepping into the choppy flow.

"We ain't gone far enough ta stop," Tater said, looking back into the blackness that bore them.

Ain't never gonna be far enough, Sully thought.

The subtle groan of the churning creek sounded, to Tater, like an evil roar building in the blackness before billowing past. It clawed at him, the tips of its soggy nails just waiting to sink into his skin and drag. It made no difference. His nervousness made the hairs on his arms prickle as if his clothes were made of cactus skins.

"We're damned," Sulley whispered.

"C'mon, Sul, north or south? Cain't just stay here til the water drops."

Sulley was caught in a trance, having fallen into the torrent of his actions, feeding the guilt inside of him that grew like wildfire on the windy plains. He heard what Tater had said, but he had no answer. He did not care. Killing a man had thrust him over a line of which he could never recover. What was done, was done. For a moment, he felt the urge to walk into the raging flow and let the water judge him for his actions.

"Sully?"

When he did not answer, Tater smacked him across the back of his head. "Snap out of it!"

Sulley stumbled forward, his hat flying into the gullywasher. "Yow-wch! Gaw-dangit, Tater. That was my best hat."

"That was yer only hat. Seein' as how ya ain't hearin' me, ya like'n ta be dead. Dead men don't need hats."

Sulley rubbed his head and watched as it sailed into the inky blackness.

"What'er we gonna do, Sulley?

"Ya 'member Lewis Preston?"

"Chewy Louie? The guy from Presidio? What about 'im"

"He tol' me once that they was hirin' hands fer ranch work near there. I say we head south an' see what we kin see, lessin' we find a crossin' that'll get us past this mess." Sulley spat into the water.

"I dunno. That's pretty close ta ol' Mexico." Tater looked back in the direction from where they came. "But maybe we don't get hung if'n we make it there."

The two shared a look, then mounted up and followed the swollen creek south. Had they spoken, their thoughts would have collided, both wrapped up in a doomsday scenario ending for the both of them. Neither lived lives that would have made a mother proud, but they were not murderers. At least not until now. Bad decisions usually led to questionable outcomes, and Sully and Tater were a mess of both.

The pair walked their horses through the dark, the weight of the day and the outcome of their deeds growing heavier with each step.

CHAPTER ELEVEN

"Stay in the wagon, Buster. No sense seein' things up close." Gid patted the young boy on his arm before climbing down from the driver's seat. His eyes were like saucers. Light from an early moon made Buster's skin look pale, as if he was overcome with fright.

"What am I supposed to do?" His voice squeaked at first but rose in both volume and intensity. "If he's dead, I wanna see. If he's dead, I gotta *know*."

Will, having tied his horse to the rear of the wagon next to Gid's, joined his brother as he talked to Buster. Gid spoke again, his tone attempting to sway the boy's insistence. "What you see here tonight ain't somethin' that'll go away. You'll carry the memory the rest of yer life, Buster."

"He's right, you know," Will said. "Don't you think you've been through enough?"

Buster slid across the bench closer to Gid and Will. He began to speak but stopped short when Sheriff Wolfe and his deputies pulled alongside the wagon.

"Come on, Henry. Let's git ta the bottom of this," Wolfe said.

Gid shared a glance with the sheriff. Even in the soft luminesce, his disapproval resounded but did little to deter the sheriff from pressing Buster further.

"Hop down an' show us where ya think he is."

Gid turned and regarded Buster. It was clear what the boy wanted regardless of the consequences that came with it, but there was nothing else he could do but help him down. Stepping back, Gid offered him a hand, but Buster did as the sheriff said and jumped from the bench. The line between a boy's innocence and a man's hard truths blurred as Buster's boots hit the ground.

"Just over here," Buster said. He took long steps, as if keeping stride with a birthing determination. "I think he's..." Buster stopped mid-step, his trailing foot raised, his arms frozen in full swing. Will and Gid followed closely, with Wolfe and his deputies in the rear. Buster wobbled on one foot, his rigid body becoming limp again as the initial shock of seeing his dead father on the ground became a gruesome truth.

"Look away, Buster," Gid said, but the young boy's eyes were locked on the body and the small, black shadows scurrying over the cooling corpse.

Moonbeams pierced through the tree branches, splitting into jagged rays like skeletal fingers scraping the ground. The pale light clawed at Cletus's dead body, echoing the frenzy of the rats' sharp teeth and tiny claws as they tore into the bloody feast.

"Will," Gid said, but he was already drawing his weapon.

In three charging steps, Will advanced on the rat-covered corpse and fired, shouting after each thundering blast. The shots caused the rats to scatter, their tiny shrieks and hisses fading as they escaped into the darkness surrounding the abandoned camp.

The sudden blasts startled the sheriff and his deputies, each crouching low and pulling their guns. Gid spun around, stepping in front of Buster before the lawmen took further action. "Put 'em down, fellas."

"What in the sam hell?" Sheriff Wolfe stammered, his wide, steely eyes alert and scanning.

"Cletus is just over there."

Straightening their stances, the lawmen holstered their weapons, though even in the dim light, their faces remained crooked, twisted with irritation, and ready for a fight.

Gid placed his hands on Buster's shoulders, his body blocking the boy's view. "You found him. Let that be enough."

With tear-swollen eyes, Buster looked up at Gid. "Can't," he said, placing his hands on Gid's and pulling them away. "Ain't a matter of what kind a pa he was, he's the only one I got." Buster wiped his eyes and nose with his sleeve.

"All right, Buster." Gid pivoted out of the way. "I'll be right behind you."

Taking a deep breath, Buster stepped forward.

Sheriff Wolfe approached and stood over the body with Will as the deputies stomped the ground, further running off stragglers of the hungry, squealing swarm. "Sure as I'm standin' here, that's Cletus Morgan." The sheriff turned and spat. "Old codger was prob'ly dead before he hit the ground."

Buster and Gid joined the men.

"You've any idea who the men were who shot yer pa, Henry?" Wolfe's voice was sharp.

The boy stared down, his gaze lost in the bloody paw prints, the shredded cloth, and the dark-stained, meaty gouge where his father's chest had once swelled.

"Buster," Wolfe said again, this time by his nickname. "What did you see?"

Buster's voice cracked, then words spilled from his mouth in an emotional flood. "I ain't seen much cause Pa made me hide in the wagon, but I heard...I heard two men. Pa said some things an' they didn't like it cause they said they'd take the wagon an' everything in it an' then..."

"Slow down, Buster," Gid interrupted.

Buster took another deep breath. When he let it out, he faced Sheriff Wolfe, his teeth clenching as a fresh feeling of anger, the likes of which he had never experienced, began to boil within him. "You gonna catch 'em, Sheriff? The men that killed Pa?"

Wolfe leaned over and spat again. "Son. I hate ta say it, but those men are long gone. Ya didn't see 'em. Sounds like yer pa didn't even know 'em."

Will and Gid shared a knowing glance.

"I can't even put papers out on 'em without a description, Buster. Best I can offer is fetchin' the undertaker and getting' ya home."

"That ain't all you can do, Sheriff, an' you know it." Gid's accusatory tone drew a snarl from Wolfe's lips.

"You best watch yerself, Mr. Crockett. Ya ain't from around here. Keepin' on like ya are, yer welcome is likely ta run out fast."

Deputy McGraw and Deputy Withers flanked the sheriff, their fingers twitching at their sides.

"In fact, you boys have helped out more than enough. We'll take it from here."

Silence fell between them, but the sheriff's words hung like thick fog. In the shadows, tiny feet scurried. Hungry eyes stared, and long teeth gnashed in hopes of another savory, fleshy nibble.

Sheriff Wolfe placed his hands on his hips and leaned forward, but Will and Gid would not be intimidated. With eyes locked on the sheriff, Gid spoke. "What do you want, Buster?"

Before the boy could reply, the sheriff interrupted. "Ain't up ta him," he said, his eyes narrowed, his voice gravelly.

"Like hell it ain't," Gid shot back.

Will's eyes flicked to the deputies as their hands shifted, resting on the hilts of their holstered guns. The air thickened with unspoken threats. He had not expected to find himself and Gid on the opposite side of the law, but as the night dragged on, it became clear that out here, justice was as thin as the wind that rustled through the trees.

Finding a steady voice, Buster stepped between the men, legs straddling his father's body. "If'n ya ain't gonna catch the men who done this, all that's left is fer me ta finish what Pa started off ta do today."

"And what might that be, Henry?" Sheriff Wolfe tilted his head to look down at the boy.

"Head on home," Buster said. "Both of us."

"What you think, Withers. He sounds just like a little Cletus Morgan," Deputy McGraw said. "Ya takin' charge now, boy?"

The words slipped from Buster like a stray bullet

fired past the deputy's ear, his message straight from the mouth of the dead. "Yer damn right I am!"

CHAPTER TWELVE

BUSTER'S CRACK SHOT ANNOUNCEMENT RICOCHETED OUT of camp and down the path and took with it the sheriff and his deputies.

"That settles it," Wolfe muttered, the words clipped and final. Without another glance, he mounted up and rode off with his deputies, leaving Buster standing over the body of his father, Cletus, with nothing but Will and Gid for company.

The boy and the brothers watched in silence as the lawmen disappeared down the trail. Gid clenched his jaw, swallowing the harsh words for what he considered a heartless act but, worse still, a dereliction of duty.

Turning back to the body, the three stood a moment longer, the brothers regarding Buster as this would be the last time he looked upon his father's face. Kneeling, Buster placed a hand on the ground, then slowly, with tentative movements, inched closer until his palm rested on his father's arm. Words fell from his lips in whispers. "Don't worry, Pa. I ain't gonna let them get way with what they done. Someday, I'll find the men that killed ya. I may not have seen their faces, but I heard 'em plain as day. It's their voices I ain't never gonna forget."

Buster stood up and faced Will and Gid. In the pale light, his face looked hardened, stripped of innocence, the first chiseled contours of manhood appearing in his gaze. "I'll bury him at home," he said, his eyes rippling with fire and dried tears. "Will you help me load him onto the wagon?"

Neither Will nor Gid answered. Instead, Gid placed a hand on Buster's shoulder and squeezed while Will walked to the wagon and led the horse nearer the body. When Buster looked at Gid, a flash of fear, resentment, and determination all balled into one glance. The boy leaned into Gid, wrapped his arms around him, and squeezed. It lasted only a moment. When Buster let go, he left what he knew of boyhood in that final hug. Stepping back, he nodded at Gid, then climbed into the wagon and began clearing space among the scattered supplies to make room for his father's body.

Will and Gid stood near the corpse, watching as Buster worked in the wagon. The boy never looked up, instead meticulously stacking and organizing what remained of the scattered supplies after the wild ride into town.

"He's takin' this rather well, don't ya think?" Gid said in a hushed tone.

"No," Will replied. "It's killing him, but it's also forcing him to grow years by the minute. Just think how we would've acted if we'd been younger when we found Ma and Pa lying in the field after the war."

Gid glanced at Buster and bit his lip. "Cain't say how I'd have felt. Mad. Hurt. All them emotions that go along with losin' someone ya love. We felt that, Will. I know I did."

"A-yuh. But the difference for him," Will said, gesturing toward Buster, "is he's got a family at home to look after now. Ain't that right?"

Gid sighed and nodded. "I'm guessin'."

"Ready," Buster said, hopping down from the wagon. He walked over and positioned himself at his father's feet. "Will, grab his arms. Gid, help me with his legs."

Gid swallowed a second thought, an offer to have Buster step aside while he and Will handled the heavy lifting. But it was clear that was not what the boy wanted. If his father's body was going to be loaded into the wagon, by god, Buster was going to have a hand in it, too.

The three moved into position. It took more bravery than Buster had ever summoned to grab and lift his dead father's leg, but he did it without complaint or any further tears. In just a couple of steps and a subtle pivot, Cletus was loaded headfirst into the wagon. Buster hopped in and covered him with a tattered burlap tarp from the wagon bed. With Cletus secured between the bag of flour and a slouching bag of beans, Buster took his seat on the bench, leaving room for Gid on his left to drive them home.

"Please," Buster said. "I need ya a little longer. Ma'll prob'ly have something for ya ta eat once we get home." He paused and looked over his shoulder. "'Cept, she ain't gonna be expectin' this."

Gid climbed onto the bench and took the reins. "We're here as long as ya need us, Buster."

The boy glanced at Will standing beside the wagon,

shaking his head in agreement, then looked at the dark path toward home. "I don't wanna be called Buster anymore," he said. "My name's Henry. Henry Morgan."

"Okay, Henry," Gid said. "Point the way, an' we'll head out."

Henry gave a whistle and called out a command in the deepest voice he could. "Walk home, Gus."

The wagon jolted and the reins stretched as the horse obeyed. The wheels squeaked and creaked as they slowly turned, rolling and bumping until the horse found the center of the trail.

Surprised by the horse's obedience, Gid turned to Henry. "By the sounds of it, you should be the one driving."

Henry's head bobbled in sync with each bounce of the wagon. "Gus is a good horse and knows the way. I just figured I'd take one last ride with my pa where I wasn't the one holdin' the reins."

Gid pursed his lips, recognizing how Henry was both letting go and stepping into a new role—one he had not asked for but was forced to accept. This was more than just a wagon ride, it was a farewell, the last ride for Henry's father and, in many ways, for the boy he had been. Gid tightened his grip on the reins, the worn leather biting into his palms, and guided the horse and wagon forward, helping Henry carry his father home for the final time.

CHAPTER THIRTEEN

An amber light flickered in the darkness, like watching eyes hidden among the trees, casting faint shadows across the front windows and slipping through the cracks in the door frame on the eastern side of the lonely cabin. It was Henry's cabin. His home. The yard was quiet except for the growl of a dog crouched at the base of the cabin's stoop.

The rickety wagon announced their arrival long before Henry could call out their arrival. As they drew closer, the door creaked open, spilling a warm, golden light onto the porch from within the rough-hewn log walls. A woman stepped through the doorway. Her movements were small and tentative, as though she expected to be noticed but held herself back with quiet caution.

"Ma," Henry called out, his tone flat.

"That you, Henry?" The woman edged her way to the porch's railing, then descended the few steps to stand beside a dog that had appeared from the shadows.

Its teeth were bared, and a low rumble of warning reverberated in its throat.

In the dim light, the woman came into full view. She looked younger than Gid had expected for Henry's mother—shoulder-length brown hair, the natural curves of a working woman, and smooth, silky skin that glowed softly where moonlight slipped through the trees above. Her stare held a frightful intensity, as if searching through shadows. But when her eyes met her son's, they softened. "Y'all about scared me half to death."

She began to approach the wagon, freezing mid-step when she noticed it was not Cletus holding the reins.

"Henry," her voice crackled as her eyes locked, rightly so, on Gid. "Where's your pa?"

Henry hopped down from the bench. The dog flinched but caught Henry's familiar scent, its growl fading as its teeth unclenched. "Ma, I...I gotta tell ya—"

Henry's mother shifted her glance to the rear of the wagon, falling first on the horse tied to the hitch rail and then to Will in the saddle. "Who are these men, Henry?"

Will pulled even with Gid. Neither said a word.

"Ma, these men are helping me."

"Helping you? How? Why isn't your father..." Her eyes fell upon Henry's as she spoke and found the answer she sought in the dried trails of tears cutting paths through the dirt on his face. She drew a deep breath, holding it as though summoning courage. When she spoke, her voice was calm. "Tell me what happened, Henry."

She placed her hands on his shoulders and listened as Henry explained how Cletus had been shot. He told how Gid and Will rode with him and stayed after the sheriff and his deputies returned to town, saying there was nothing they could or would do to try and catch the killers.

Will and Gid watched, then felt the brunt of Henry's mother's heavy glance. She shook her head, brushing away the remnants of unsuppressed emotion. "You two looking to get something out of this?" she said, her eyes flicking between Gid and Will, her words sharp with accusation. "We don't have money, and I don't—"

"Pardon the interruption," Gid said, "but no, ma'am. We ain't looking for nothing like that."

Pivoting Henry around to stand in front of her, with hands still firm on his shoulders, her voice remained defensive. "Aren't many a man, especially in these parts, that don't have something to hide, or lies they're used to telling."

The rumbling growl from the dog returned, echoing the woman's mistrust.

Henry pulled away and turned to face his mother. "They ain't like that at all."

"You're just a child, Henry Morgan. How could you know that?"

Henry stepped forward and took her hand.

His gentle squeeze and unwavering stare showed what he had said, and what he believed was true. "I *know*, Ma."

She pulled him close and wrapped her arms around him. Pressing her eyes and clenching her jaw, she fought back a tide of swelling emotions, some of which swirled with guilty feelings. When she opened her eyes again, they fell on the men, on Will and Gid, and were more accepting of their presence.

"My name's Liza Morgan." She swallowed the rising

lump in her throat as she shifted her gaze to the bed of the wagon. "If you'd be so kind as to pull the wagon around the side of the cabin. Don't want my girls to see what you're carrying."

Gid nodded. "Yes, Ma'am."

Will followed Gid as he parked, then dismounted and tied his horse next to Gid's at the rear of the wagon.

"She's holdin' back," Gid whispered.

"What choice does she have?" Will replied.

"Come inside when you're ready," Liza said. "I'll put some water on for coffee."

She released Henry from her embrace, climbed the steps to the porch, and headed straight inside. Henry remained at the top of the cabin's stoop, waiting for the brothers. The dog stood guard at the base, a warning growl gurgling louder as they approached.

"Don't mind her," Henry said. "She's mostly all talk."

"Mostly?" Gid said, stopping when the dog bared its fangs.

Henry hopped down the steps and crouched next to the dog. A gentle rub along its back and a scratch behind its ears stilled the growl, its bared teeth slipping away. It sat back on its haunches, lolling its long pink tongue from the side of its mouth.

"See, she's harmless."

"That's cause she knows yer in charge," Will said.

Gid stepped forward and knelt in front of Henry and the dog. It watched with guarded eyes as Gid slowly extended his hand, letting the dog catch his scent. Its nose twitched, then bumped Gid's hand, accepting him and requiring a friendly scratch to seal the deal. Gid rubbed the dog's head. "Yer right, Henry. She's not so bad." Gid slid his hand along the dog's side and, after a gentle pat, stood up and smiled at Henry.

"Come on inside," Henry said. "Now that she knows ya, she won't show teeth again."

Henry and Gid made their way up the stairs, Will following behind and the dog bringing up the rear. At the top of the steps, Will turned to the dog. "What's her name, Henry," he said, bending down with an open hand.

"I call her Saba."

Will lowered his hand further.

"But Pa called her Killer."

Will froze, eyes locked on the dog, then retracted his hand, deciding to let it warm up to him on its own.

Henry pushed the door open and held it while the brothers walked inside. "Stay, Saba," Henry said.

The dog sat, then turned to face the yard and slunk down to its chest, laying its head on its front paws.

As Henry shut the door, Liza approached Will and Gid with a tray holding two steaming cups of coffee. The rich aroma filled the air, mingling with the warmth of burning candles and the soft glow of embers in the fireplace. They each took a cup then found a seat around a small wooden dining table offset in the corner across the room. As they sat, two new faces appeared, peeking through a doorway that led to an interior room.

"Looks like we have company," Gid said.

Liza turned and saw her two young daughters hovering in the shadows, eyes wide and curious but still unaware of their family's loss.

"Girls," Liza said. "If you're gonna show yourselves, might as well come all the way out."

Dressed in tattered nightgowns, the girls scurried

past Henry and huddled around Liza, latching onto her arms.

"Faith. Grace. These men..." Liza stopped, her breath catching in her throat.

"They're my friends," Henry said. "Gid and Will Crockett, but ya best call 'em Mr. Crockett."

The girls shared a glance, then pinned their eyes on their mother. As if in practiced rhythm, they both asked, "Where's Papa?"

CHAPTER FOURTEEN

FEAR PUSHED SULLY AND TATER ONWARD, BUT HUNGER, exhaustion, and a rare stroke of luck finally forced them to stop running for the night. Their southward trek brought them to a shallow crossing where the rushing creek thinned out over a broad expanse of smooth, scattered stones.

"Holy hell, Sully! I'm spent," Tater said.

Landing on the far side of the creek, he dismounted and led his horse to the water's edge for a drink. Kneeling, he dipped his hand into the cool shallows. The runoff trickled over his fingers, soothing in another time or place, but not in the dead of night, and not while they were on the run. He scooped a handful to his mouth, the chill biting his teeth, then wiped his dripping chin with a dirty sleeve and glanced around.

Sully remained in the saddle, unmoving, his eyes fixed on the black void of the West Texas plains stretching endlessly before them. The sky sparkled with stars, clustered in places to form a heavenly stream that seemed to divide the dark from the light—or perhaps the bad from the good. Tater glanced back at the rippling water they had just crossed, the faint current shimmering under the starlight, and wondered to which side they truly belonged.

Standing, he saw movement among the watery stones. He squinted, catching a sudden flash of silver that was different from that of the reflective water. "Sully. Hop down an' com'ere."

Sully turned his head, his face drained of color, his cheeks sagging as his mouth hung open.

"Damn, Sul. Git on over here. I think I found somethin'."

Sliding out of his saddle, Sully joined Tater at the water's edge.

"Look," Tater said, pointing.

"Ain't nuthin' but wet and dark, Tater." Sully's voice dragged.

"Shoot, Sully. Yer so gawl-danged tired ya cain't even see where yer lookin'."

Tater marched through the shallow stream, each step sloshing and squelching under his boots. He crouched as he approached the flashing silver, then whirled around and raised his arms in victory.

"Oh, we lucky on this one, Sully. I found us some eatens."

Sully's stomach was in knots. He was far hungrier than a simple grumble would suggest, and now, with the prospect of having something inside his belly, he jumped at the chance to eat.

"Tell me it's a bag er satchel filled with somethin' good, Tater."

Tater crouched, then stabbed his fist into a shallow

tide pool, splashing water over his legs before pulling his hand back. When he opened it, Sully's heart sank and his stomach lurched as if receiving a punch to the gut.

"What the hell am I supposed to do with that?"

Tater pinched his fingers around the tail of a tiny minnow and held it between them. "Ain't much, but'll fill us a bit if'n we catch more."

Sully looked into the tide pool, cut off from the main flow and holding a small school of tiny fish.

"Thems too small ta cook." Sully looked at Tater, then glanced around. "An' we ain't got nuthin' fer a fire even if we did find one big enough."

Tater clenched his jaw. "This is survivin', Sully. Ain't nothin' else ta do but pinch yer nose an' swallow."

Sully watched as Tater lifted the minnow in front of his face. It wriggled once, flopping in a futile attempt to escape, but Tater held a firm grip on its tail. Shrugging and closing his eyes, Tater opened his mouth, tossed the minnow onto his tongue, and gulped.

"Well?" Sully asked.

Tater shuddered, gagging once before recovering. "Ain't so bad. I seen a Chinese fella eat worse that time we were in Galveston. Slurped fish and other tiny creatures like they was rock candy from the general store."

Sully looked into the pool, his eyes following the tiny fish darting back and forth, their scales reflecting the silvery light of the moon.

"Go on," Tater said. "Git ya one."

Sully took a knee, then hovered his hand over the water. Before diving in, he looked up at Tater. "Don't ya ever speak of this beyond tonight. Hear me?"

Tater nodded, licking his lips like a hungry wolf.

Sully turned his gaze back to the water, flexed his fingers, and plunged them into the school of tiny fish.

CHAPTER FIFTEEN

INNOCENT TEARS FELL WHEN LIZA EXPLAINED, IN TERMS safe for a child's ears, what had happened to their pa. The girls' tiny wails turned to whimpers in her arms as she comforted them. Henry stood by the fireplace, poking the last embers and watching sparks rise into the stone chimney.

"Settle down now," Liza said, squeezing the girls. "You best get some sleep. There'll be lots to do when you wake up."

She stood with the girls still latched on to her and skillfully maneuvered the three of them through the doorway, out of sight. Even from the other room, their muffled cries stabbed at Will and Gid.

Gid swallowed the last of his coffee, then placed his cup on the table. "Can't let this one go, Will." He shifted his gaze to look at Henry and spoke in a quieter voice. "That boy, this family deserves more."

"We bounty hunters again, Gid?"

"I reckon we are, 'cept this time there ain't no payout at the end."

From the porch, a low growl rose to a steady rumble, followed by a sharp warning bark. The brothers and Henry all shot looks at the front door.

"Saba!" Henry said, heading for the door.

Will and Gid stood.

"What's got ya riled up this time?" Henry continued.

"Hold up," Gid said, intercepting him as his hand touched the door handle. "Give 'er a minute."

Saba's growl penetrated the wood, her warning as steady and sharp as when they arrived with the wagon.

"Git behind me, Henry," Gid said. His eyes flicked to Will's, then he eased the door open to have a look. Saba stood, nose pointing into the dark beyond the wooded yard. Sensing movement behind her, she twitched, then bolted from the porch, jumped from the stoop, and shot into the trees at top speed. Gid stepped onto the porch with Henry and Will close behind. Groundcover rustled under Saba's paws, the sound enabling Gid and Will to track where the dog was going.

Henry pushed past Gid to run after his dog but was pulled back by Will before he had the chance.

"Don't know what's out there, Henry."

Out of the dark and chased from their hunt by Saba, a volley of yipes and barks rose out of the woods.

"Ki-yotes," Gid said.

"Probably smell the—" Will stopped short, but his meaning fell on everyone. Henry's shoulders sagged. He sighed, shifting his gaze to the wagon where his father's body lay covered and still.

"We outta bury Pa. Tonight."

Will and Gid shared a knowing glance. Henry's words were heavy, humbling, and his unexpected transformation continued to surprise them. It was a suggestion that an adult should have offered, but circumstances evolving as they did led Henry to make one of the biggest decisions of his life.

"He's right." Liza's voice carried beyond the front door where she now stood, her gaze following Henry's as his eyes were still glued on the wagon. "But I want to see him first. Clean him up a bit."

Will turned around and shook his head. "That's not a good idea."

"I don't care if it's a good idea, Mr. Crockett. Cletus Morgan, hard a man as he was, still provided for us. He was my husband." Liza crossed her arms, her voice firm. "And it's what he deserves."

"I think what Will's sayin'," Gid said calmly, "is that maybe ya should remember Cletus how he was before. Shotgun blasts don't leave a pretty sight. Ain't no different with yer husband, Ms. Liza."

The yipes and barks continued as Saba chased the coyotes further from the cabin.

Tearing his gaze away from the wagon, Henry walked to his mother and put an arm around her waist. "Maybe," he said, turning around to face the brothers. "Maybe you could cover him except for his face." He looked up at his mother. "Would that be enough, Ma?"

Liza leaned over and kissed the top of Henry's head. "Yes. I believe it would," she said. "There's a small shed out back. It should have the right tools to..." Liza paused, swallowing a wave of rising emotion. She squeezed Henry tighter before letting go. "To dig a grave. Henry will show you."

Without another word, Liza whirled around and disappeared into the cabin.

"You can just tell us, Henry. We'll do the rest." Gid said.

Henry walked to the porch rail and looked up toward the tops of the trees and the black sky beyond. "No. Ain't yer job alone, but I could still use yer help."

Not waiting for a reply, Henry took to the steps, then rounded the corner at the near side of the cabin.

"Come on, Gid," Will said. "Sooner we get the body in the ground, the sooner everyone can move on."

Will and Gid caught up with Henry at the shed. It was dark, but the boy knew where everything was and, after a few clanks of metal, quickly produced two shovels and a pickaxe.

"Here," Henry said.

"These will work just fine, Henry," Gid said, taking hold of one of the shovels. "Where should we dig?"

"Pa always sat on a stump closest ta an old Live Oak at the edge of the property. I think that'd be the best spot."

"Lead the way," Will said.

As they started back, Gid's gaze strayed to a rear cabin window. A candle on the sill lit the room, its hot light magnified by the glass. Inside, Liza stood clutching a white cloth, her shoulders trembling in quiet convulsions. It was a moment meant for her alone, and Gid knew he should look away, but he hesitated. She wiped her eyes, composed herself, then turned and froze when she saw him watching. Their eyes locked briefly before she stepped out of view. Gid felt a flush of guilt. He had not meant to intrude, but her quiet strength and momentary vulnerability stirred something deep in his chest, a mix of guilt and empathy he could not quite shake.

"Damn," Gid whispered to himself as he hurried to catch up to Will and Henry.

They disappeared around the front of the cabin when Saba's growl returned to the edge of the porch and became a ferocious bark. Raising the shovel in front of him like a loaded rifle, Gid ran to catch up.

"Ki-yotes back already?" he said, rounding the corner, nearly barreling over Will and Henry, who had stopped dead in their tracks.

"Nope," Will said as Gid stumbled to a stop. Shapes emerged from the shadows. Men on horseback, their rifles catching the faint gleam of moonlight. "Coyotes don't ride horses—or carry guns."

CHAPTER SIXTEEN

SULLY LAY ON HIS BACK, EYES WIDE AND LOOKING FROM bright star to bright star. The wide expanse of West Texas spread out in all directions, the horizon slipping into shades of black darker than the deepest pit. There was no fire, no real warmth to speak of, except the burning in his gut. Cramping from their earlier unconventional meal, it felt as if those tiny fish swam about inside him, bumping, nibbling, wriggling around in search of a way out. His nerves were a wreck, and sleep avoided him like he was the ugly girl at a barn dance.

He pulled the collar of his duck cloth jacket around his neck, the weathered fabric not long enough to cover his ears from the chilly night air, and tried counting stars to help him fall asleep. It was no use. Tater had drifted off, his light snoring intensifying into a deep sawing grind. Sully kicked his boot and tossed a handful of gravel at him, but neither effort woke Tater. He grunted, rolled onto his side, and mumbled within an indecipherable dream.

Succumbing to frustration, insomnia, and the churn

in his stomach, Sully sat up, then stood and walked to the water's edge. The wide stream rippled, its melodious tune everlasting. The rocks and water played a soft duet, but to Sully, it was a static that he could not turn off.

Stepping ankle-deep into the flow, his leather boots deflected the water as he leaned down, cupped a handful, and sipped from his palm. The drink settled his stomach a little, but a sense of misdirection hovered over him, punishing him with questions for which he had no answers.

Where the hell are you going, Sully?

He stood and wiped his dripping hand across his chin.

You can run, but do you honestly think you can ever escape what you've become?

"And what's that?" he yelled, his voice carrying over the plains before being swallowed by the night. His mind spun like a whirlwind, making it hard to decipher if what he thought he had heard was real or just his mind playing tricks.

You're...a killer, Sully. There's no going back.

His heart thudded against his ribs, each beat a reminder of the life he had taken and the blood that would not wash clean, no matter how long he stood in the water.

He twisted, stomping his feet and splashing his pant legs. With clenched fists, he swung his arms like a man brawling with shadows, memories—unforgiving ghosts of regret and desperation dragging him to his knees.

"I ain't...a killer!" he yelled, swinging wildly at the air. Shuffling his feet, he tripped on a large stone in the pebble-strewn wash and tumbled hands first into the runoff.

Yes...you are.

Beaten down and forced to his lowest, Sully crawled out of the water. Mud caked beneath his fingernails and filled the cracks in his skin like paste.

A sharp breeze blew past, carrying with it a change in Sully. Its crisp bite sank into his skin beneath his wet clothing. It scratched at his face, scarring him with a raw desire to quell the cold. The cramping in his gut eased. As he stood, he arched his back and rolled his eyes into his head, colorful stars bursting behind his eyelids. Lifting his arms over his head, he stretched and groaned like a bear disturbed from hibernation, his fingers flexing outward as his head tilted back. When he straightened, a twitch at the corner of his mouth curled his lips into a snarl.

He took a step, wobbling at first, then another, until he stood over Tater at their cold camp. Sully looked down at his brother, then scanned the horizon in all directions. The plan had been to head south and find work, but in his fractured mind, every card was back on the table. He continued to twist his body around until he faced west and saw a yellow flicker in the distance. A soft glow, perhaps a campfire.

"There," he said, his voice sounding different, the word *feeling* different. "Get up, Tater."

When Tater did not move, Sully kicked him in the side with his boot.

Tater grunted, rolled away, and grabbed his ribs, glaring at Sully. "What'd ya go an' do that fer?"

Squinting at the distant light, Sully let his thoughts grumble in his throat.

Tater scooted back and pushed himself upright. "What's got inta ya, Sul?"

"There's ground ta cover," Sully said, his eyes wide and more intense than Tater had ever seen.

"Hell, Sully. It's late, an' I don't—"

"Shut yer mouth, Tater. Mount yer horse or stay behind."

The growl in Sully's voice caught Tater by surprise. He had never feared his brother before, but the way Sully was acting now concerned him. "Com'on, Sully. Let's wait and ride out at first light."

Ignoring him, Sully walked to the horses, unhobbled their legs, and grabbed the reins. "Last chance," he said, the whites of his eyes filling his sockets as his ultimatum hung in the air.

Tater stood, brushing himself off as he watched his brother like he was looking at a stranger—a man touched by something darker than exhaustion. Conceding, he walked over and grabbed the reins to his horse out of Sully's hands. "Them fish musta swam from yer stomach to yer brain, cause yer actin' goddamn crazy, Sully."

Sully grinned, his discolored teeth showing through the gap of his lips. Without a word, he turned and stepped into the stirrups. Planted in the saddle, he reined his horse west and aimed for the distant, snapping glow.

"Ain't crazy ta embrace the storm, Tater." Shouting, "He-yaw," he kicked his heels and took off. Tater followed, the haze of sleep, the shock of Sully's sudden change, and confusion about where they were headed clouding his judgment, sealing his fate beneath the starlit West Texas sky.

CHAPTER SEVENTEEN

THE SHARP GLINT IN THE RIDERS' EYES MATCHED THEIR crooked scowls as they sat tall in the saddle, rifle barrels aimed at the sky. Will squinted, his eyes darting from one man to the next. Four in all, they lined up side by side, like the harbingers of pestilence and ruin, an ill omen cast upon the Morgans' land. The third rider in line nudged his horse forward, his face emerging in the fractured streams of silvery moonlight.

"It true, what they been sayin' 'bout Cleuts?" he asked, his voice low and gravelly, his eyes locking onto Will's.

Behind Will, Henry made a move to push past Gid, but Gid intercepted with a calculated sidestep and a firm forearm, halting the boy in his tracks.

"Keep yer head," Gid whispered, his voice barely audible, his eyes fixed on the riders' every move.

Will shifted his weight, his boots crunching on the ground. "Little late to come calling, don't ya think, friend?" he said, his tone steady though the tension in the air was thick enough to cut.

The man leaned over and spat. "Little late is right, 'cept we ain't the ones bein' late. Cletus Morgan owes us. All of us, an' we intend ta collect. S'posed ta be from him last week, but he ain't anteed up." His eyes slid from the house to Henry, a menacing grin spreading across his face. "We ain't opposed ta settlin' with whoever's left."

"Guessin' ya didn't hear my brother," Gid said, his voice calm yet firm. "This ain't a good time, mister. Why don't y'all turn around an' head on outta here."

The man turned his attention to Gid, a slow sneer curling his lips, then lowered his rifle and pointed it squarely at him. "From where I'm settin', it don't seem like yer in any position ta make demands."

Will shifted his gaze to the riders flanking the man. They too had trained their guns on Gid, their hardened faces unyielding.

"You Cletus's boy?" the man said, gesturing with his rifle to Henry.

Henry put his hands on Gid's arm like he was caught behind a porch railing. He swallowed hard before he spoke. "It's like we already said. Y'all just git."

"I ain't takin' no sass from you, boy," the man grumbled and began to dismount.

BLAM!

The horses jumped, and the outsiders jolted in their saddles, but their focus snapped back to the porch just in time to see the cabin door slam shut. Liza stepped out, shotgun smoking in her hands, and smoothly shifted her aim from the treetops to the riders. "Y'all heard my boy. Best be on your way. Don't know what's been said in town, but Cletus is dead. Whatever debts he had died with him," she said, her voice forceful, commanding the moment.

The man adjusted himself in the saddle, cocking his head at her with a slow, deliberate sway. "Men die. Debts don't," he said, each phrase carrying a weight of its own.

He glared at Liza. The stillness between them hung heavy, broken only by a faint rustling beyond the trees. Then came a low, insatiable growl, rumbling up from the base of the porch.

Out of the corner of Gid's eye, he saw the blackened swirl of fur and night blur together as Saba bolted from its spot and charged the horse and rider closest to the cabin. With two lunging strides, it leaped at the side of the horse. The whites of its fangs and eyes flashed like tiny bolts of lighting as the dog sunk its claws into the horse and its teeth into the leg of the intruder.

The dog's actions sparked the dry, heavy air, causing instant chaos in the yard. The three flanking horsemen flinched, turning their guns toward the dog, but hesitated. Only a perfect shot would kill it without injuring the rider. In that moment, Will pulled his pistol and took aim. Gid grabbed Henry and yanked him back until he was at the edge of the cabin, then charged forward, shovel in one hand, while pulling his pistol with the other.

Saba clenched down, her teeth like a bear trap on the man's leg just above his boot. The horse stomped and turned causing the rider to struggle for balance in the saddle. He looked as if he were riding a bucking bronc, one hand waving in the air, unable to gain a solid grip on the rifle it held, the other gripping the reins and pulling back hard, attempting to control his steed.

The blackened flash and sudden surge happened in an instant, but in this storm, lighting followed the thunder.

Reining his horse to one side, Saba's body twirled outward as the circular movement of the horse forced its hind legs to sail outward. The fourth rider, closest to Will, took aim and fired at the dog as it flashed past him. His shot missed the dog but splintered a section of wood railing nearest Liza. Will fired at the man, hitting him in the shoulder. The shot knocked him back in the saddle, but he did not fall to the ground. Gunfire erupted, sharp and chaotic, like the burst of a fireworks finale.

The two other riders turned their aim toward Will and Gid. Will jumped sideways and rolled, bullets tearing into the ground where he had just been. Gid dodged left and hurled the shovel like a javelin at the man struggling with Saba, hitting him with the dull blade along his elbow. The blunt force did not break skin, but it did dislodge the man's grip on his rifle. Retreating to the edge of the cabin, he shielded Henry as the fight escalated.

Empty-handed, the man screamed, his eyes wide and angry, then pulled a machete from a saddle scabbard and held it high above his head like a headsman before an execution. As he slashed downward, his arm halted midway, the blade tearing from his grasp as an explosion from the porch caught him in the chest and threw him back off the horse and onto the ground in a mangled mess of blood and bones.

Liza ducked as another plume of fresh smoke swirled around her shotgun's barrel. Indecisive blasts from the remaining men on horseback clattered in the air, painting easy targets for Will and Gid. With three bursts from Will, the first rider toppled out of the saddle, his left ankle caught in the stirrup. His horse bolted, dragging the man into the dark past the cabin. The sound of his body skimming along the brush faded into the night.

"Stay put, Henry," Gid said. He pulled himself onto the porch and hopped the railing, running toward Liza and yelling. "Get down!"

Gid advanced with his pistol outstretched, each stride marked by a flash of flame and the harsh stench of gunpowder. The cylinder clicked and rotated after each shot until all chambers were empty and the once-seated bullets pierced the air.

Liza buried her head in her lap and covered her ears as Gid slid in front of her. Three of his six shots hit, each true bullet burying itself in the last rider from his throat to his hip. The man dropped his rifle and clutched his neck as warm life pulsed from him. His last gaze found Gid's, his eyes seeming to glaze further with each final beat of his dying heart. He slumped in the saddle like a discarded ragdoll, then sluffed to one side and fell with a dull thud on the ground.

A sudden quiet fell upon the cabin like a gust of chilly north wind. Saba climbed the steps and ambled over to Liza, tongue lolling to one side and lips seeming to curl upward as if she knew she had been a good girl.

Gid slowly stood, then turned to Liza. "Ya, okay?" He offered a hand to help her to her feet.

"Where's Henry?" she said, looking past the bodies in her yard.

"He's fine. Safe. Tucked over by the corner of the house," Gid said.

Liza followed Gid's finger and saw her son crouching and peering around the wooden beams. Relief consumed her, then immediately bolted when her gaze fell upon the splintered decking and dime-sized holes in the cabin wall.

"The girls!" Liza rushed to the door and disappeared inside the cabin. Gid scanned the yard, looking for Will. He saw him standing over the man who had acted as the intruder's leader and had threatened Liza. Out of the corner of his eye, Gid sensed movement and turned to see Henry walking from the cabin toward Will.

For a moment, Gid considered stopping him. The boy had experienced a lifetime of trauma in only a few short hours, why subject him to the gruesome after-math of his first, and hopefully last, gun battle? But Gid did not stop him. There were lessons to be learned, and Henry was now the man of the house. His young eyes had little choice but to face the world as it was.

Henry's steps were tentative at first, then equalized into a normal gait. Gid stepped off the porch and joined Will at the same time as Henry.

"You recognized these men, Henry?" Will asked.

Henry looked down at the body, then raised his head to look across the yard at the other men. Moon-light cascaded through the trees like miniature spot-lights, their spackled beams looking like a decorated church at Christmas.

"Henry?" Will said, his voice soft, patient.

He turned away from the bodies and looked toward the cabin. "No, sir. Not a one."

Liza stood on the porch. A lock of hair dangled over her cheek, separating bravery from worry. Henry's younger sisters clung to her waist, their arms wrapped around her like a braided belt.

Without another word, Henry stepped around the dead man's body, bent over, and picked up the shovel that Gid had thrown. He turned back to the brothers, his face absorbing a silvery swath of light, then gave his mother a sideways glance. His eyes looked deep, shining like tiny blazes in the night.

"Sooner we git Pa in the ground, the sooner we can figure out what to do next."

CHAPTER EIGHTEEN

WHAT WAS ONCE BUT A CANDLE FLICKER IN THE DISTANCE now glowed with flames rising and rolling, dancing in the crisp air above the crackling fire as Sully and Tater approached the lonely camp. A single horse picketed near the perimeter acknowledged their presence with an uncomfortable snort. An empty bedroll stretched out on the ground beyond the fire, its lumpy folds and crumpled creases looked as if it had recently been vacated.

Without waiting for an invitation, Sully urged his horse forward, stopping only when the pale light of the late moon mingled with the flickering glow of the fire. Tater, who had not spoken to Sully since leaving the water, opened his mouth to voice his objections about entering the camp uninvited. He never got the chance. The metallic slide and sharp ratchet of a rifle round seating in the chamber shattered the silence of the night —a distinct and unmistakable warning to halt their approach.

"Sully," Tater said, his voice hushed and uneasy. "Ya hear that?"

"He heard it, fella." With his rifle raised and aimed at the brothers, an older man walked from behind the horse. "Ain't proper helpin' yerself inta another's camp."

Tater watched the man with the rifle, his eyes tracking the barrel as its muzzle swayed between him and Sully. Red suspenders stretched taut, holding his pants snug around his waist. A soiled, long-sleeved undershirt clung to his chest, tufts of gray, curly hair poking through the gaps where the buttons hung open. A felt hat sat low on his head, an eagle feather tucked into the leather hatband. Scraggly hair above his ears thickened into bushy lambchop sideburns that trailed down his cheeks. His chin and upper lip were clean-shaven, yet a layer of grime darkened his skin, giving him a rough, weathered appearance.

Sully's lips parted as he drew a deliberate breath, exhaling with a sharp whistle through his teeth. Leaning forward in the saddle, he rested an elbow on the horn and let a slow smile spread across his face. "Well, ya ain't wrong about that, mister. My apologies," Sully said, removing his hat with an overt gesture of subservience. "Let me find some words that might settle yer nerves."

The man squinted his eyes as he lifted his chin. "No sense in searchin' fer somethin' that shoulda been there in the first place. You'll understand if I ask ya ta be movin' along."

Tater spoke up, his voice stuttering at first. "Yer...yer right, mister. We ain't oughtin' ta, ya know—"

"Would you just shut up," Sully interrupted,

swiveling in the saddle to glare at Tater. "The man don't need ta hear yer blabber."

Prickles ran down Tater's spine, spurred by the sudden glint in Sully's eyes. His expression, hidden from the man holding the rifle, made Tater grow more uneasy with each passing second.

Sully continued, his back turned away from the man. "I dunno, mister. It's late an' getting' chillier, an' yer fire is so invitin'." He watched Tater's eyes until they flicked away from his, widening as his gaze landed exactly where Sully had hoped.

"No," Tater mouthed, though atop his horse, he was too far away from the man to show his tell.

Sully had slipped his hand from the saddle horn to his waist when he turned to chastise Tater, his palm settling on the hilt of his revolver. Staring at Tater, his fingers flexed, his teeth clenched—all within a single charged moment. He spoke to the man as he turned, his voice sharp and apologetic, laced with a nastiness Tater had never heard before. "We'll be on our way," he said, his tone dropping lower with each word, even as he drew his gun and fired.

The man reacted with a single shot, the round flying wide as Sully's bullets ripped into him. Each malicious blast drove him back, tearing into his chest, his arm, the meat of his gut. His rifle slipped from his grasp as he shuddered, fighting a losing battle to stay upright. Tater let out a scream, raw and panicked, like a child thrust into his first fistfight. Sully, however, remained still, soaking in the moment. He inhaled the charred air, his gaze fixed on the man as he crumpled to the ground.

"S...Sully? What have ya..." Mouth wide with shock, Tater was unable to finish his thought.

Displaying a gunfighter's skill, Sully slid his weapon into its holster with surprising ease, then slowly turned to face Tater.

"Looks like camp is abandoned after all, Tater. What d'ya say we hop down an' warm ourselves by the fire?" He grinned, then dismounted and helped himself to the crackling warmth, rubbing his hands together before hovering them near the flames. "C'mon. Gonna need ta stoke this one up if'n it'll last 'til first light."

Tater's gaze lingered on the lifeless body sprawled on the ground. The man's back arched awkwardly, propped by his left leg, twisted beneath him in death. His mouth hung slack, thin red streaks of blood tracing lines down his chin. Glassy eyes stared skyward, as if transfixed by something far greater than anything he could have imagined.

"I'm damned," Tater whispered as he reluctantly climbed off his horse. He glanced at Sully, now tending the fire as if nothing had happened. A hollow pit opened in his stomach. "Worse still," he muttered under his breath. "I'm trapped."

CHAPTER NINETEEN

THE GROUND NEAR THE TREE STUMP THAT HENRY HAD chosen to bury Cletus was hard-packed and riddled with dead roots, but neither Will nor Gid complained. Henry kept to himself, working alongside the brothers, matching their pace without letting up.

Wielding the pickaxe, Gid struck the earth again and again, loosening the soil and cutting through the tangled web of buried roots. Will and Henry each manned a shovel, scooping and digging. Even under the blackened sky, where the temperatures felt cool to the skin, beads of sweat dripped from their foreheads. The chosen plot was not ideal, but it was Henry's decision—a fitting one in its own way. The ground was as obstinate as Cletus: unforgiving and stubborn.

After an hour of moving earth, they had reached a depth that was sufficient to protect the corpse from wild animals.

Gid knelt next to the freshly dug hole and grabbed a handful of dirt, squeezing it in his palm until it sifted through his fingers. The cool earth released a fresh, farm-like smell, rich and familiar. It reminded him of newly plowed fields back home in Missouri—a memory that, in turn, awakened the nightmare of finding his father shot and killed and his mother lying nearby, naked and dying. She had died in front of him just as Cletus had for Henry.

"What do you think, Henry?" Will said, resting his hands on the end of the shovel.

"I think it's time to get my mother." He looked at his palms, raw and blistered. "Can you... Will you carry him for me?" he said, his voice finally taking its turn to crack as the reality and weight of the day could no longer be set aside.

"Do what ya need ta do, Henry. We'll handle everythin' out here." Gid said, still kneeling.

Henry nodded, then silently turned and walked to the cabin carrying the shovel he used to dig his father's grave.

"Ya think he'll be all right?" Gid said, watching him go.

"It'll take some time, but he's already changed right before our eyes," Will replied. "The bigger problem is what comes next for all of them."

"Yeah." Gid said, standing up. "Considered that. If Cletus had debts ta pay, more 'n likely, he had more owed than ta just these men tonight. An' with every minute we spend hangin' around here, the ones who killed him git further away. How'd we find ourselves on both ends of the same tug-a-war rope, Will?"

"Don't matter. We're here now. Liza seems strong enough to fend for her family. Ain't up to us to protect them, but we did tell Henry we'd track down Cletus's killers. Come first light, we all should hit the trail."

The sharp slap of the cabin door jolted them into motion.

"C'mon," Will said. "Before they come out."

Gid wiped his hands on his pant legs as they walked to the wagon to retrieve Cletus. The brothers were strong, and together, they made quick work of moving the body to the edge of the grave. It was rigid—a sight no one, least of all Henry or the girls, should have to endure, no matter what kind of father or husband Cletus had been.

Cletus's open chest wound had fused to the burlap, the dried blood sticking like glue. As they carried him, the sickening sound of stretching cloth tearing away from plastered skin and bones was a visceral reminder of the gruesome injury Cletus had sustained.

After placing his body on the ground, Gid returned to the wagon and brought back another portion of fresh, unstained burlap and covered Cletus from head to toe.

"That oughta give him some dignity," Gid said, his voice low, "while easing the sight of him for the rest. Don't ya think?"

Will nodded, turning his head at the sound of footsteps clattering over the cabin porch. "They're coming," he said.

Gid stepped beside Will on the far side of the grave, Cletus lying at their feet. At any other funeral, they might have looked like pallbearers—men of honor, ready to escort the dead to rest. But they were neither close friends nor family. They were strangers, bound not by kinship but by a quiet sense of duty, determined to see justice and reverence served.

It was late. Not the ideal time for ceremonies meant to be given their full attention, yet with more corpses than anyone would care to look at lying across the property, there was no time like the present. The sooner Cletus was laid to rest, the sooner Liza and the children could make a plan for themselves.

With a daughter in each of his mother's hands, Henry followed them from the cabin to the gravesite. Still too young to fully understand what had happened, the girls cried quiet tears, mourning the loss of their father. Liza held a firm upper lip, her face awash with emotion, though not entirely attuned to sadness. Beneath it all, there was a hint of relief. Her cheeks were flushed and dry.

Liza stopped short of the grave, the girls buckling in her hands not expecting the sudden stop. "Let's get on with it," she said.

The girls' eyes darted from the body to the hole, then, in unison, their gaze returned to Liza, full of questions and confusion.

"Do you want to say anything?" Will asked.

Liza looked away and swallowed. When she turned back, her jaw was clenched tight, as if holding back a flood of words she refused to voice.

"I'll say something," Henry said, stepping around his mother to stand between her and the Crockett brothers. He looked at his feet, his toes perched over the edge of the fresh hole. Raising his head, he glanced at Gid. As he spoke, his gaze shifted, finally locking on Liza. "Pa weren't always the easiest ta understand. He had his ways about 'im. He was tough, on me mostly, but I figured it was on account of losing my older brother an' needin' ta teach me how ta grow up faster than I oughta." Henry paused, forcing a smile. "In his way, he loved us all, I reckon."

Liza nodded, her eyes growing bloodshot, her heart swelling with pride for the young man standing in front of her.

On her left, Grace tugged at her hand. "Is Pa gone for good?"

"He is," Liza said, looking down at her.

On her other arm, Faith chimed in, her words trailing into the night, intentional, yet half-spoken. "No more yelling."

Liza took a deep breath and exhaled. "If you want to say anything religious-like, be my guest. Cletus wasn't what you'd call a god-fearing man, but seein' as his soul is under judgment..." Her eyes lingered on his body, hidden beneath the burlap throw. She tightened her lips for a moment before adding, "Maybe he needs a little something to help him along."

Henry turned to the brothers. "Either of you know what ta say?" Earnestly, his attention rested on Gid.

"I s'pose I might have some words worth speakin'," Gid said. He cleared his throat and shuffled his feet, then bowed his head. "Lord, I did not know this man, but when I look at his family, he must have done something right. No one deserves to leave this world before their time. Those Cletus left behind should take comfort in knowing there's a plan, even if we don't see it now. Ain't none of us know what that means except it is in faith that we accept what has happened. It says in Ecclesiastes 3:1, 'To everything there is a season, and a time to every purpose under heaven.' His time here is done, and now he stands before You. Judge him with fairness, Lord. And grant peace to the family he left behind. Amen."

"Amen," Will echoed, then patted Gid on the shoulder.

Henry and Liza repeated in kind, the girls mumbling their reply with hung heads.

The silent moment between family and strangers and the dead in the night was broken by rustling in the trees. Albeit a raccoon or opossum milling about, its sudden noise brought an end to the brief ceremony.

With a cordial nod to the brothers, Liza turned and led the girls back to the cabin. Henry stayed back, looking down at the black hole in the ground.

"Why don't ya run along, Henry," Gid said. "Me an' Will can finish up here."

Henry nudged his foot forward, knocking a clump of dirt into the grave. The dull, soddy thud of earth on earth drummed a single beat of finality.

"I'll stay," Henry said.

Working quietly, Will and Gid lifted Cletus and eased him into the hole, careful not to drop either end. Filling the grave was a much easier task, but each scoop of dirt was placed with a delicate hand. Regardless of how Cletus lived his life or treated others, Will and Gid acted as though he were a special person to Henry, even though it was clear that he was far from that.

As the hole filled and the body was buried, Henry approached Will and reached out to take the shovel from him.

"Here," Henry said. "I want to finish on my own."

"You sure about that, Henry?" Will said before letting go.

Henry nodded and Will released his hold of the shovel, then stepped back out of the way. Gid joined him and watched as Henry scooped the last of the misplaced dirt and spread it over the fresh mound.

When he finished, Henry turned to the brothers. "All this on account of a pie contest. Bet ya never imagined things turnin' out the way they did today," he said.

"Henry," Gid replied, stepping around the grave to stand toe-to-toe with the boy. "Seems like every day is like that. Some are good. Some are bad. Ya just have to play the hand yer dealt the best ya can."

"God's honest truth, Henry," Will added. "The thing you need to hold onto now is how will you face tomorrow. It's likely to be just as challenging as today."

"Will it get better?" Henry asked.

"Only if you allow it to, Henry," Will replied.

Turning toward the cabin, shadowed lumps of dead bodies on the ground with riderless horses standing in effigy haunted the night. Forgotten during the burial, their presence now loomed like a warning. The question was not if more men like them would come calling —but when.

CHAPTER TWENTY

WITH THE PASSING OF MIDNIGHT, THE MOON SLIPPED below the horizon, leaving behind a soft glow that stretched across the land in an endless, silver ripple. Tater sat facing the murk, concentrating on the highlights of a dying moon. He could feel the warmth of the fire on his back, but inside, a coldness remained.

How long is Sully gonna keep this up? he wondered.

A sudden surge of garbled snores erupted near the campfire where his brother had sprawled out to sleep. Tater twisted around, disgust contorting his face at the sight of him. Sully's hat covered his eyes, his mouth agape and jaw slack in deep slumber. His legs stretched out with feet propped up on a saddle once belonging to the man they had met upon arriving at camp.

Tater shifted his gaze to the dead man. He, too, lay still, untouched where he had fallen, unchanged except for a tinge of pale gray creeping over his skin.

Poor bastard. Prob'ly woulda invited us in, had we gone about things differently.

Tater turned back around, his chest heavy and

uncomfortable, his mind racing with thoughts, though none made sense to him.

He rubbed his eyes, exhausted, but sleep was a prize far beyond his reach tonight, stolen by the weight of damage done and the uncertain road ahead.

CHAPTER TWENTY-ONE

W<small>ILL AND</small> G<small>ID STOOD WITH</small> L<small>IZA ON THE PORCH, THE</small> late hour advancing with the setting moon behind the trees.

"You have any place to go until things cool down?" Will asked. "Bound to be more men looking to claim what they feel Cletus owes 'em. With word already spreading around town about his death, it may not be safe for you and the kids here all alone."

"You don't even know Cletus," Liza answered. "How could you expect more men?"

"Don't have ta know 'im," Gid said. "Me an' Will have known many men just like 'im. Ain't but a few that don't spread themselves around. Most of the time, dead beats..." Gid paused, absorbing a surprised glance from Liza. "What I mean ta say is, it becomes easy ta dig a hole of debt ya cain't climb outta. It's likely Cletus made deals with more than one devil."

Liza crossed her arms and shivered, her body reacting to a mix of cool breezes and the prospects of harsh reality. Looking over her shoulder, she peered through the front window to see Henry sitting alone.

"That boy in there," she started to say, pausing to settle a rising lump in her throat. "He's not the same as he was this morning. I look at him, watch him, and I see someone older than he is, yet still wearing a boy's body."

"Liza," Gid spoke with a softness in his voice, daring to empathize with a mother's right to worry. "I only met Henry this afternoon, but what I've seen in him since then reminds me of men on the battlefield. At first, they're scared of everythin', an' rightly so. But as the battle rages on, some of 'em take to the action. They embrace it. Hell, some look for more than they should. With Henry, I see some of the same traits in those brave soldiers. I don't believe he'd back down from anyone threatenin' you or his sisters. He ain't my kid, but if he were, I'd be more concerned about how he'd react to the next round of collectors."

Liza sighed, each word hitting hard, but she saw it as well.

"I've got a cousin in Amarillo we can stay with for a while. Truth be told, I only followed Cletus out here because he was my husband. Convenient as it was at the time for both of us, it turned out to be a mistake. Money was hard to come by. It affected Cletus in many ways. Made him crass, short-tempered, sometimes..." Liza's words trailed off as if struck by a bad memory. Falling captive by her thoughts, her mind drifted until she realized she had left things unspoken. She shook her head and squeezed her crossed arms tightly to her chest. "Anyway. Losing Cletus hurts, but it may not be the worst thing in the world. I hate to admit that, but I can't help but feel like a weight has been lifted off my shoulders."

Will and Gid did not speak. Instead, they looked out from the porch, observing the tree line, the trail leading to the cabin, the scattered bodies.

"If I might suggest," Will finally said. "We can help load the wagon with things you and the children need. First thing in the morning, you should head into town and get on the next train bound for Amarillo."

"And what about you?" Liza asked.

"Us?" Gid replied. He glanced at Will, then answered her question. "Will and I are headed after the men that killed Cletus. The sheriff ain't havin' nothin' by it."

"Why?" she asked, stepping closer to Gid. "What's in it for you?"

Gid cocked his head. "Not a thing. Will an' I ain't ones ta let things fester, though. We figure findin' the men might help Henry, that's all."

Liza turned and placed her hands on the porch railing. "I can't say I've ever met men like the two of you."

"Aw, we're not special," Will said, testing the mood with a lighthearted remark. "Especially not Gid." He paused as Liza turned around, her face betraying her with a subtle smirk. "We just know what it's like to lose someone, an' how it feels when justice is served, that's all."

"Well, it still seems a little...peculiar," Liza said. "But then again, nothing about today has been ordinary."

The cabin door opened, and Henry stepped outside.

"So, we're leavin'?" he said, walking over to Liza.

"It looks that way, Henry."

He glanced sideways, pointing to the nearest dead man. "What about them?"

"Let the marshal deal with 'em," Will said. "Swing by the sheriff's office on your way to the train depot. Tell him what happened. Wolfe can file his report and pass it along to the marshal's office. Might even have a look for himself, but since it happened outside of town, and how he already dismissed the idea of catching Cletus's killers, I reckon he won't bother much."

"An' by the time they do look inta it, y'all should be long gone," Gid added.

"We got money for the train?" Henry asked.

Liza looked at him, then leaned over and kissed his forehead. "Don't worry about such things, Henry Morgan. It's not your place."

"Besides," Gid said, drawing Henry's attention. "The tickets are already paid fer. All ya have ta do is ride inta town an' pick 'em up."

Henry squinted one eye, thinking. "How—"

"You head inside and get some sleep, Henry," Liza said. "We have a lot to do in the morning."

"Yes, ma'am," Henry replied. He turned and headed for the door, pausing a moment to look back. "Will. Gid. Thanks fer...well, everything."

The brothers nodded, and Henry went inside and closed the door.

"The tickets are already paid for?" Liza asked in a low voice.

"Look, Liza," Gid said, pulling a wad of bills from his pocket and reaching out to her. "It's more than enough to see you all the way to Amarillo."

Liza pushed his hand back. "We'll make do."

Gid glanced at the wagon, remembering the sparse

supplies Cletus had purchased. It was obvious she needed the money but was too proud to take it.

"Tell you what," Gid said. "Consider it a down payment on the cabin. Yer not comin' back any time soon, are ya? I mean, didn't ya say that movin' out here was a mistake? Let me an' Will take it off yer hands. We can settle the balance once we catch Cletus's killers. Until then, you have some cash, an' we have a lead on a huntin' cabin. An' if'n ya want ta come back, say the word an' ya can pay us back then."

Liza took a deep breath. "I don't know. Everything is happening so...fast. And, really, we just met. How can I..."

"Trust us?" Gid said, finishing her sentence.

Liza nodded.

"Actions, Ms. Morgan, speak louder than words. I think we've earned a bit by now," Will said.

"I'm sorry," she said. "You're more than right. Everything you and Gid have done has been admirable. You haven't asked for a thing. It's just hard to believe someone, or two in your case, would make such a selfless gesture."

"It ain't selfless if it makes the giver feel good, Liza. Me an' Will, we wanna help."

Liza's gaze bounced back and forth between the brothers. Their gentle smiles and nodding heads making her more comfortable with the offer.

"All right," she said.

Gid reached out the handful of money, and this time, Liza took it.

"Consider yourselves on the way to owning a hunting cabin, though," she said, looking away from the porch. "I'm not sure what you would want to hunt around here."

"Rabbits," Gid said without missing a beat. "Long-eared rabbits."

The ridiculous comment was well-timed, injecting a bit of levity into the moment. Liza let a laugh escape her, and Will rolled his eyes, smiling.

"Everythin' is gonna be all right, Liza," Gid said.

Liza's smile fell into flattened lips as the reality of her situation returned to the forefront of her thoughts. "I hope you're right, Gid," she said. "I hope you're right."

CHAPTER TWENTY-TWO

As the sun cracked the horizon, golden beams spilled through the trees, revealing a wagon loaded with supplies and four passengers preparing to depart.

"That didn't take as long as I thought," Liza said, standing with Will at the base of the cabin porch. "You'd think picking up and packing your life away would result in more than you could handle. Truth is, we didn't have much to begin with."

They watched Gid and Henry help the girls into the wagon for the ride to town. Faith yawned, still groggy from being roused so early, while Grace was chipper, humming an aimless tune, her innocence untouched by the sudden change, oblivious to the potential dangers lying ahead.

"Even if the wagon were empty, you have everything you need right there," Will said, nodding toward her children.

Once the girls were settled, Henry hopped down and walked around the wagon, listening to Gid as he was reminded to always double-check the load for shifting cargo and that the axles held enough grease. After circling and inspecting the wagon, they joined Will and Liza.

"Looks like yer ready ta hit the trail, Liza," Gid said.

"Thank you, Gid. And you, too, Henry." Liza smiled at her boy, her eyes softening as they fell back to Gid. "Will you be seeing us into town?"

Henry, standing tall, cut in before Gid could answer. "I know the way."

Liza pursed her lips before answering. "You're absolutely right, Henry."

"We'll tag along until we come to the..." Gid paused, fishing for a word or phrase, doing his best to avoid saying *the spot where Cletus was murdered*.

"'Til we pick up the tracks were lookin' for," Will added, stepping in to save Gid.

Liza glanced between them, her gaze lingering on Gid as if sensing there was more to the story. "How will you know?"

"It won't be that hard," Gid said. "Spend enough years trackin' beasts an' men, an' ya learn to read the signs like a book."

Bird calls from within the trees and the crackles of branches bending beneath the weight of scurrying creatures rising with the sun orchestrated a farewell tune to Henry and his family as he and his mother loaded up and pulled the wagon away from the cabin.

"Will we be comin' back?" Henry said, his voice hushed so his sisters would not hear.

"I don't know, Henry. One day, maybe." Liza rubbed Henry's back, then folded her hands in her lap. Henry looked back, "Almost forgot," he said. Liza turned to look when Henry whistled, then called out, "Saba, come on, girl."

Crawling out from under the porch, the dog stretched out its legs and yawned. Straightening, it gave Will and Gid a glance and licked its chops, then trotted off until it caught up with the departing wagon.

Will and Gid mounted up, their gazes sweeping over the sun-bathed aftermath of last night's gun battle.

Gid cast a hard look at each of the dead men. Their horses, ground tied near the lifeless bodies, stood indifferent, as though waiting for their riders to rise. "It's good we were here," he said.

"Yeah," Will agreed, nodding. "Things coulda been a whole lot worse."

"Worried their bodies'll attract scavengers?" Gid asked.

"They might, but I ain't worried about it one bit. Those men knew better than to harass Liza and her family, but they did it anyway, and before Cletus was even in the ground."

"A-yuh. Just what I was thinkin'."

The sun continued to climb, its rays casting a crown that pulsed with a golden glow around the cabin, plunging its wood frame into a shadowed silhouette, as if hiding it from the dangers of the world.

Will and Gid shifted in their saddles, the fingers of morning touching their backs with a silent warmth. Before them, Henry drove the wagon away from the cabin and the only life he ever knew.

"C'mon," Will said. "No sense in hangin' back. Let's catch up with Henry and the girls. Ain't too far until they pass where Cletus was shot."

Will nudged his horse along. Gid followed, riding next to his brother.

"Ya think we'll find the men who killed 'im?"

"It'll be like tryin' ta find a couple of red-headed prairie dogs hidin' in the middle of one of those West Texas digger towns," Will said, shaking his head. "The odds ain't too good."

Gid nodded, a smile brimming across his face. "But, there's a chance," he said. "With you an' me, Will, there's always a chance."

The trail to town was well worn with grooves cut over time by regular travelers. The terrain rose before opening into a wide field, a transition marked by scattered brush and patches of grass, lined with mesquite and taller elms, their branches swaying in the early morning breeze. It was also the spot where Cletus met his demise.

Noting the area, Gid signaled Henry. "Let's hold up, Henry."

The girls jostled in their spots as the wagon slowed to a stop. Will and Gid circled their horses around to stand face-to-face with Henry and Liza.

Gid spoke first. "Sun's gettin' higher. Town ain't too far off. Ya good ta drive 'em on by yerself, Henry?"

Henry glanced over his shoulder, his eyes widening as he recognized where they were. Forcing them into a squint, he returned his gaze to Gid. "We'll be fine," he said.

Henry set the brake and extended his hand. Gid took it without hesitation, his larger grip firm, shaking it as he would for any man who had earned his respect.

"Yer in charge now, Henry. The man of the house,"

Gid said, letting go. "But remember, it's okay ta be a kid every once in a while."

Those words made Liza smile.

"Liza," Will said, tipping his hat. Turning his attention to Henry, they shook hands as well.

"Am I ever gonna see y'all again?" Henry asked.

"I'd say so," Will replied. "One of these days,"

"You bet," Gid agreed. "Once we catch the men we're after, me an' Will might just make our way through Amarillo. We've been wantin' ta head north anyhow."

"Do be careful," Liza said.

"Yes, ma'am," the brothers answered in unison.

"Go on, now, Henry. Get yer family safely ta the train depot," Gid said.

"And Liza, when you stop to talk with Sheriff Wolfe, be just as careful with what you say," Will suggested. "He doesn't need to know y'all are leaving town for good. Just that losing Cletus and the trouble at the cabin last night left you needing to spend time with your cousin until things settle down."

Liza nodded, understanding the implications.

Will and Gid backed their horses away from the wagon. Henry released the brake and called out to their horse, "Walk on."

The wagon jolted once, its old wooden frame groaning under the strain before settling into rhythm with the horse pulling Henry and his family toward town.

Under blue skies, Will and Gid watched until they were out of sight.

"All right, Gid," Will said, looking at his brother. "Time to track down men we can't describe, who fled in a direction we don't know, across miles of unforgiving land, with nothing but a hunch and whatever signs they were careless enough to leave behind."

"Oh, is that all?" Gid joked. "We've had less ta go on before. At the very least, we've got a startin' point."

Will shifted in the saddle, raising his hand to cover his eyes. "True. Let's spread out and see if we can't find some tracks worth following."

CHAPTER TWENTY-THREE

THE BRIGHT BLAZES OF MORNING STUNG TATER'S bloodshot eyes, weary from little sleep and weighed down by the growing anxiety that had festered within him through the night. He sat at the edge of camp looking west, wondering where he and Sully might be headed today. Too engrossed in worry and fighting exhaustion, he did not notice footsteps approaching from behind.

Sully's shadow stretched across the terrain, looming large beneath the West Texas sun, growing longer with each step until it swallowed Tater whole. Standing behind his brother, he pressed a boot against Tater's back and kicked, shoving him into a forward, discombobulated roll.

Tater grunted as he tumbled, a final "*Ooof*" forced from his lips when his body crumpled to a halt.

"Good ta see yer awake, Tater. Thought fer a second there ya mighta been somewhere else. Ya know, in the head." Tater looked up to see Sully circling a finger next to his ear.

Tater squeezed his eyes closed. *I ain't the one who's fled the coop.* Keeping the thought to himself, he pushed up from the ground, patted his legs and hands to remove the loose dirt and dust from his clothes. When he straightened, Sully's stare was waiting.

"What the hell, Sully?"

"Nothin'." Sully raised his hands like pistols, firing off finger bullets at Tater with tiny, whispered explosions, a mocking echo of their childhood battles. His wild eyes tracked the invisible shots, as if watching them tear through soft flesh. "Gotcha again. Yer dead, Tater."

Holstering his imaginary guns, he spun around with exaggerated flair, arms stretched wide, before coming to a stop. His gaze landed on the dead man sprawled near the ashen fire ring.

"Woo-ee. That stench. Smells like somethin' gone bad—real bad." He took a step forward, then pointed. "Is that what I smell?"

Tater bowed his head, then tilted it just enough to watch Sully through hooded eyes as he sauntered over to the ripening corpse and delivered the same kick he had given Tater. The body toppled to one side, unnatural and rigid, like a crooked scarecrow knocked from its roost. A sickening, dull thud followed as the man's forehead and chest rammed the ground. Blackened, crusted puddles stained the earth where the body had rested since last night.

Tater looked around, found his horse, and contemplated getting the hell out of there, but it would be a futile escape and would only worsen things between them. Like it or not, Sully was his brother, and that meant Tater was not going anywhere but with him.

Sully stood over the body, looking down on it as if waiting for it to move on its own.

"Dead. Dead. Dead. That's what ya are, mister." Sully turned around and took a knee next to the man's saddle and dug into a leather satchel attached to the horn. "Wonder what he's got fer eatin'."

Tater approached, his belly rumbling, his pride itching, but the chance for real food outweighed all else. He glanced at Sully, then to the bag in which he was rummaging.

"Find anythin'?"

Sully ignored the question, his digging becoming more violent as he pulled and tossed one thing after another from the bag—a tin flask teasing of whiskey long gone, a boned pocketknife, a well-used flint and steel, a compass with cracked glass, a tin of salve, a tattered Bible with dog-eared pages, a small mirror, and an empty water skin.

"Christ all mighty!" Sully stood with the bag in hand, then spiked it on the ground. "What's a man doin' this far out without anythin' ta eat?"

"Maybe he done et it all already?" Tater said. *Or maybe he's like us. On the run without a plan?*

"Son of a bitch!" Sully stomped around the fire pit, his voice echoing the same phrase over and over like an ill-tongued mantra. At once, he stopped, then turned and marched over to the picketed horse. "What say you, huh?" he yelled.

The horse knew what Sully was before he ever reached the tether—danger. Its ears pinned back, and every muscle in its body coiled, ready to flee. With flared nostrils and eyes like saucers, it stomped its hooves and pulled against the leather binding, bending but not breaking the picket to which it was tied.

"Let 'er be, Sully. Ain't doin' no good shoutin' at a horse, anyhow."

Sully whirled around. "Yeah? Well, it's makin' me feel better."

"Maybe the fella was on a short trip. Maybe he lives 'round here an' didn't need ta carry so much along?"

Not finished with his tirade, Sully turned on Tater. "Ya got an answer fer everythin' now, huh? How abouts ya fix us some breakfast. Use yer wits an' all that what ya got upstairs." Sully punched a finger at his temple as he stomped closer to Tater.

"Settle down, brother," Tater said, his voice teetering between pleading and exasperation. "Let's mount up an' keep headin' west like we talked about."

"Nah." Sully shook his head, edging closer. "That ain't what we're doin' now. We gonna turn it around. I figure there's men that owes us. Hell, the last saloon we been at took us fer more than what's fair. I think we pay 'em a visit and reclaim what's ours."

"What's gotten into ya, Sully. I ain't never—"

"Ya ain't never been a real man, Tater? That what yer gonna say? Or was ya gonna say somethin' about me?" Sully stopped, nose to nose with Tater. "Ya know, I kin see it in yer eyes. Ya think I've changed since killin' that man with the wagon, an' ya'd be right about that."

Sully took a step back and began pacing back and forth in front of Tater.

"Before, when we was wanderin' from place ta place feelin' helpless an' hungry, I ain't have it in me to do fer myself what I thought others should. Now, even if by accident, killin' that man awakened somethin' in me I cain't explain except ta say..." He stopped pacing, locking his fiery eyes with Tater's. "I like it. I like it a lot."

Seeming to find a sliver of calm amid the storm, Sully reached forward and laid a hand on Tater's shoulder.

"Next one's on you. Time ya find out how freein' it is ta kill something bigger than you."

His grip slipped to Tater's neck and tightened.

"In fact, why don't we have a little lesson about that right now. Call it a warm-up before the big show." Spittle flung from his lips as he talked. "Let's see if ya got it in ya."

Turning, with his hand gripping Tater's neck like a horse collar, Sully pulled him along.

"Let go, Sully," Tater said, trying to shake free.

Sully squeezed tighter, his nails digging into skin. "Stop yer whinin'. Ya sound like a little girl."

Sully dragged Tater past the fire pit, then yanked him to a halt to face the open range of West Texas beyond the camp, and the dead man's picketed horse.

"There," Sully said. "Should be easy enough." He let go of Tater's neck and pulled his pistol from his belt. "Use my gun, Tater."

"What?"

"Ya hard of hearin'?" He shoved the pistol into Tater's chest. "Take the gun, an' shoot the horse."

Dread washed over Tater, its chill stabbing him like jagged icicles against bare skin. With weighted reluctance, he raised his hands and fumbled with the weapon until it fell into his grasp.

Sully stepped back, his lips curling, the corners of his eyes carving crow's feet halfway to his hairline.

He cradled the weapon like a first-time father

holding a newborn, unsure and awkward. It was not the gun that caused his hesitancy, but Sully's expectations.

"I can't," Tater said, his voice quiet and wavering.

"Do it. Raise that hog, an' blast that horse ta smithereens. It's tied down. Ain't goin' anywhere's. It's a sure shot, Tater. A sure thing."

Sully stepped next to Tater. Pressing his hands beneath Tater's arm, he lifted the gun until it was level with the horse. "There. All ya gots ta do is pull the trigger."

"Sully...why? What the hell will killin' that animal prove?"

Sully let go and stepped between Tater and the horse. His eyes cut like slits, his lips held firm, showing a thin line of gritted teeth in its gap.

"It'll tell me if yer yellow. If yer with me or not."

Sully rolled his head, the crackles in his neck causing Tater to flinch.

There's no way...no way!

Then, a clarity broke through the haze, offering a single out for Tater. A way to be free of the unsettling man in which his brother had so rapidly transformed.

It ain't right. It just ain't...I can't do that either...

"Now," Sully demanded, his voice low and growling.

Tater positioned the gun, its sights set on the beautiful white strip of muzzle hair, just to the right of Sully's head.

"One way or another, yer pullin' that trigger," Sully warned. "I'm gonna count ya down."

Tater swallowed.

"Five..."

His fingers curled tighter around the grip, the cold

steel biting into his palms. The barrel shook, its iron length growing heavier.

"Four..."

Sweat beaded on Tater's brow, a single rivulet of fear-soaked terror trickled over his skin until clinging to the edge of his pointy chin.

"Three..."

Tater's mouth turned to sand. "Sully, I..." What breath he had escaped, causing his chest to burn.

"Two..."

"Please," he mouthed, but there was no negotiating with the devil that had become his brother. The barrel swayed left, then right, like a pendulum ticking away the seconds before disaster, his hands too unsteady to hold it still.

"One..."

A single heartbeat drummed in Tater's ears, the echo rumbling like distant thunder.

Jesus, help me.

BANG!

CHAPTER TWENTY-FOUR

THE SOFT CLOMPS OF HOOVES AND THE OCCASIONAL whinny of the cart horse echoed through the quiet as the wagon clanked into the far end of town. At this hour, everything was calm. Clarendon, Texas, the only town Henry had known growing up, seemed smaller this morning than he remembered.

Liza sat quietly next to him, her brow furrowed in thought, consumed by the steps she must take to ensure her family's safety. Faith and Grace huddled together in the bed, asleep in each other's arms like puppies snuggling, their heads wobbling with each rock of the wagon. Henry glanced back at them and smiled, their peacefulness a gift compared to the unease pressing on his chest.

The row of buildings along Main Street loomed ahead, connected by a wooden boardwalk that clattered like horseshoes under hurried feet during busy days but now lay silent. Even the saloon stood still, its batwing doors hanging motionless as if frozen in time. Before, all these details would have gone unnoticed by Henry, but this morning, everything felt different. *He* was different. Not only had his life changed overnight, his perception of the world around him had shifted as well.

Henry guided the wagon past the church. The leather reins, worn soft and stretched thin from years of use, felt smooth in his grip. He nodded at the town preacher, who stood at the water well near the church square, pulling the rope hand over hand to draw a fresh pail. Henry sighed. It was the same spot where he had planned to meet Mary Sue to watch the fireworks, but that felt like a distant memory now, a time when he was still innocent and most people called him Buster. The preacher paused to smile, acknowledging Henry's nod, before resuming his morning routine.

Remnants of yesterday's party still lined the streets —ruffled cloth banners draped along the boardwalk railings, broken bottles and discarded handbills littering the gutters. Stray papers clung to snags in the wooden walkway and the weeds sprouting beneath. Ribbons and burned fireworks casings lay scattered on rooftops and across the dirt-trodden street. Festive decorations had turned into morning eyesores, simple trash waiting to be cleared away and forgotten.

Like the dead men at the cabin, Henry thought.

As they approached the sheriff's office, Liza laid a hand on Henry's knee. "Take us to the depot first. Once we've got our tickets and the wagon's unloaded, I'll head back to talk to Sheriff Wolfe."

"What about the wagon? And the horse?" Henry asked. "Maybe we should take her along. We could pay for her in the stock car, couldn't we? Anyhow, she trusts me."

"Freight costs money, Henry. Money we can't spare right now."

"But the wagon," Henry argued. "I can sell it to the blacksmith. We can use that money for the horse, an' then, when we git ta Amarillo, we'll have somethin' ta haul what we brung along."

Liza pursed her lips, looking long and hard at her son. How grown he seemed this morning. It was not right. It was not his position to be making such suggestions, and yet, it had become so. "Henry Morgan, anyone ever tell you how smart you are?"

Henry looked at his mother, a warmth of pride simmering in his stomach.

"If there is time once I finish with the sheriff, you can take the wagon with the horse and try to sell it, but if the blacksmith makes a bargain for both, the horse goes too, agreed?"

The horse's ears twitched, actively listening to the voices behind her while continuing to pull the wagon toward the depot at the opposite end of town.

"Yes, ma'am," Henry said, his hopes hanging on a deal he had yet to make.

A few moments later, they arrived at the depot. Henry parked the wagon near the loading dock and set the brake. The halting wagon jostled the girls in the bed, waking them and causing Faith to bump her head on the sidewall. She groaned and rubbed away the pain but was no worse for wear.

"Look after your sisters," Liza said. "And start unloading. I'll run and see if the ticket office is open and when the first train through Amarillo will arrive, and then go talk to the sheriff." She paused, then placed her hands firmly on Henry's shoulders, leaning in so her words would not be missed. "And, Henry," she said, her voice low but steady, "Like Will and Gid said, no one needs to know we're not coming back. If anyone asks, tell the truth, but leave that part out. Got it?"

"Yes, ma'am."

Liza climbed down from the bench and headed toward the ticket office, her steps brisk and purposeful. Henry hopped into the back of the wagon, his boots landing with a thud on the wooden planks.

"Come on, sleepy heads," he said to his sisters. "Help me git this stuff onta the loadin' dock."

Faith continued to rub her head. "Where's Mama?"

Henry smiled as he reassured his sister. "She'll be right back," he said. "Then you an' me an' Grace an' Ma will all git on the train an' go for a ride. That'll be fun, huh?"

"Okay," Faith said, stretching with a yawn.

Henry reached for a burlap sack in the wagon bed, its rough twine cinched tight around a bundle of quilts, a skillet, a stack of tin plates, and a small collection of spoons. "Grab that sack," he said to Faith, nodding toward the smaller bag near her feet.

Grace clutched her doll, its painted face smudged from years of love, as she stumbled sleepily to the wagon's edge. "What about Mama's Bible?" she asked.

"I got it here," Henry said, patting the worn book tucked into the crook of his arm.

He worked quickly, pulling a warped wooden crate from the wagon. Inside, the contents shifted as he hefted it onto the dock.

"Another one down," he muttered, more to himself than to his sisters.

"Don't forget our bag," Grace said, pointing.

Henry paused, placing his hands on his hips. "I thought y'all were helpin'."

"We are," Faith insisted. "We're making sure you don't forget anything."

Henry shook his head and got back to work. Leaning over, he hefted another small trunk, packed with his few clothes and the things most important to him—a pocket knife his pa never knew about, a slingshot he had made from elm branches and rubber strips he had found in the trash heap behind the livery, and a half-carved chunk of hackberry, its form only beginning to look like a sculpted deer. He set it carefully with the rest before returning to see what was left.

Behind him, Faith and Grace sat on the edge of the dock, their feet swinging idly. Faith clutched the sack of beans, waiting for her brother's next instruction.

"Pass me that one," Henry said, pointing to a smaller bundle near Grace's feet.

Faith scrambled over and dragged the bundle closer to the edge. It held a few odds and ends—spare clothes, a tin of lard, and fabric scraps Ma had insisted on bringing. Henry took it with a quick nod of thanks and added it to the pile.

Finally, he reached for the last of their supplies: a dented bucket with a few stray tools rattling inside. The handle was splintered, but he figured it might come in handy once they reached Amarillo. He placed it gently on the dock beside the other items and stepped back.

"All right, girls," Henry said, brushing the dust from his hands. "That's the last of it. Now we just wait for Mama."

The soft creak of the wagon's bed settled into silence, but another sound began to emerge: the steady knock of boots against the wooden planks of the loading dock. At first, the children did not notice, their minds still lingering on the task they had just finished.

But as the dense thud grew louder, Henry's ears pricked, and he turned toward the sound.

A figure approached, the sun at his back casting a long shadow across the dock. Henry squinted, his breath hitching slightly as the outline of a large man came into focus. The stranger's bulk blocked the sunlight, leaving his face in shadow.

Henry straightened, stepping between the man and his sisters. Lifting his chin, he spoke, his tone confident, respectful. "Can I help you, mister?"

CHAPTER TWENTY-FIVE

GID KNELT NEAR THE FRONT OF HIS HORSE, HIS HAND hovering above faint markings in the dirt. The morning light highlighted the unblemished impressions, their sharp shadows resembling scattered puzzle pieces across the ground. One by one, he traced their shape with a fingertip, his eyes narrowing as he studied the tracks. "Over here," he called out. "Ain't no doubt these are what we're lookin' fer."

Will reined his horse toward his brother and slid out of the saddle. His boots crunched on the dry ground as he walked to where Gid knelt. "Whatcha got?" he asked.

"Two sets of prints," Gid said, standing and motioning to his left. "They start there." He turned, tracing an invisible line with his hand as he pointed west. "See how deep they dig? Whoever rode these horses was in a rush, likely spooked by somethin'. The prints level out farther on, like they fell into a run."

"Could be anyone," Will said, scanning the tracks. "What makes ya so sure these are the ones to follow?"

Gid walked a few paces to the spot where they had

found Cletus's body. The earth was darkened with blood, still visible in dried smudges despite the scuffle around it. He pointed to the ground nearby. "Follow the footprints."

Will swept his gaze across the mess of tracks. The area was a maze of impressions—boots, hooves, and scuffs blending into a chaotic web of movement. He shook his head. "Too many, Gid," he said, "Looks like someone held a damn barn dance right here."

"Yer gettin' rusty, brother," Gid said, a smile tugging at his lips. "Look closer an' you'll start ta see the patterns." He moved around behind Will, his eyes fixed on the dusty impressions in the ground. "Forgit about these," Gid continued, gesturing with his hands as though sketching an invisible picture. "Check yer boots. Them prints are likely ours from when we walked in ta collect Cletus. Ya see how they stride in, then shuffle out nearly the same way?"

Gid stepped to his left, circling across from Will. "Forgit these, too. Them smaller prints have ta be Henry's. Ain't no grown man got feet that small." He straightened and looked at Will, his voice steady. "Ya startin' ta see?"

"A-yuh," Will said, his brow furrowing as the pattern unfolded in his mind. "That means the rest belong ta Cletus an' the two men that killed him."

Will turned, following a pair of bootprints that trailed away from the scene before vanishing at the edge of the trail. "Okay, Gid. These must be Cletus's. No other reason fer 'em ta stop right here, except he jumped down from the wagon. See here? You can spot the tracks an' the skid marks where the wagon bolted like a bandit, headin' for town."

"That leaves two pairs left ta follow," Gid said, hunching his back to lean closer to the ground. His eyes darted through the jumble of prints, piecing together the story: the interactions, the struggle, the gunshot, and the final escape. He followed the retreating tracks to the tree line, where deep hoof marks tore into the dirt. From there, he traced the route back to the spot that had first caught his attention.

"Yep. It's them fer sure," Gid said, rising.

Certain of his brother's skills, Will stepped through the old tracks to join him, his eyes locking onto the trail the killers had left behind. "Good work, Gid."

"C'mon, Will. Mount up," Gid said, nodding toward the trail. "We're headin' west."

CHAPTER TWENTY-SIX

THE HORSE SCREAMED, SQUEALING LIKE A STUCK PIG, ITS nostrils flaring with terror as it lunged and pulled violently against its picket.

Smoke rose from the barrel like puffs from a signal fire, jagged and sharp with each convulsive twitch in Tater's hand. The report of a single shot dwindled, its echo folding into the vast silence of the West Texas plains.

Hooves pounded the earth, kicking up dirt until, SNAP! The stake splintered, and the horse bolted, galloping into the open horizon.

"Damn it, Tater! Ya cain't do anythin' right," Sully spat, storming toward his brother.

Snatching the gun from Tater's hands, Sully cocked the hammer and took aim at the fleeing animal.

"No!" Tater shouted, ramming Sully's shoulder just as he pulled the trigger.

The bullet sliced through the air, veering wildly off course. A second shot ripped through the stillness, shattering it like fragile glass.

"Son of a bitch!" Sully bellowed, stomping the ground. He spun around, his face twisted with fury as he leveled the gun at Tater.

"Look what ya did, Tater!"

"Me?" Tater stammered, his voice rising as his eyes darted between Sully and the threatening barrel of Sully's gun.

"Yeah, you!" Sully snapped. "That horse was a dead giveaway, Tater. Now, when it shows up wherever it's goin' without a rider, someone might wonder why."

Tater's jaw dropped. He was not a smart man, but even he knew there were better ways to handle the situation than killing an innocent horse. "We shoulda just taken it with us," he muttered.

"What? I ain't no damn horse rustler, Tater?" Sully sneered, lowering the gun. "Ya know a man gets hung fer stealin' horses."

Sully turned and spat, his eyes fixed on the faint dust trail the horse left behind.

An' he won't for killin' a man? Tater thought, the words boiling silently in his throat.

"Still, Sully," he said aloud. "We coulda—"

"Shut up, Tater." Sully's voice was sharp, ending the discussion with a tone that brooked no argument. He marched past his brother, snatching the saddle bag he had rummaged through earlier. "Grab what ya can. We'll sell it once we're in town."

"Town?" Tater asked, confusion flickering across his face. "I thought we was headin' south. Escapin'. Disappearin'. Don't ya remember?"

"The plan changed," Sully said, his voice low and gravelly. He let out a rattling growl of frustration. "We got a score to settle with them Faro dealers in Tascosa."

"Tascosa?" Tater's face twisted in disbelief. "That takes us back north—right past where we kilt that man! We'll get caught fer sure."

"I ain't scared of gettin' caught no more, Tater, but if yer feelin' yellow, we'll swing wide so's we don't double down our tracks. We'll head west fer an hour, then due north. We kin cut back south of Amarillo an' slide right into Tascosa clean as a whistle." Sully smirked, his eyes narrowing as he stepped closer to his brother. "Ain't no one lookin' fer us, dummy. Plus, who'd think we're stupid enough to head back toward the scene of the crime?"

Tater scratched his jaw, unease creeping into his expression.

"What's the matter, Tater? Don't ya trust yer brother?" Sully's voice dripped with mock sincerity, his hand settling on Tater's shoulder.

Their eyes locked, a silent battle raging between them. In an act of strained concord, Sully tightened his grip. "Well?"

Tater swallowed hard, forcing down the knot in his throat. "I trust ya," he lied.

"Good," Sully said, his lips curling into a thin, satisfied smile. He turned and began collecting scattered supplies, stuffing them back into the bag. He then walked over the man and picked up his hat, which had fallen when Sully shot him. He placed it on his head and turned to Tater. "What d'ya think?"

Sully's smile curled into a scowl when Tater did not answer.

"Grab the saddle. We'll sell it at a tradin' post lessin' we find someone ta buy it along the way." Sully then picked up the man's rifle, still lying where it had been dropped. Holding it before him, he spoke to himself, marveling over the weapon. "But I'll be keepin' this fer myself. Winchester 1873. Now that's nice."

Pleased with his trophy, he slung it over his shoulder like a soldier and marched to his horse. He wedged it between his bedroll and the leather strap, holding it snug against the cantle, then swung onto the saddle.

Tater hesitated, glancing toward the horizon where the horse had disappeared. A part of him wished he could run as it had, fleeing the weight of what they had done, what his brother had become. But Sully's voice was sharp and commanding and Tater had nowhere else to go. "Move it, Tater!"

Grumbling under his breath, Tater hoisted the saddle, the weight of it dragging at his shoulders as much as his doubts dragged at his heart.

CHAPTER TWENTY-SEVEN

HENRY STIFFENED, STANDING AS TALL AS HE COULD between his sisters and the very large man who stood before them on the loading dock. Without having said a word, he stood like a rugged oak, his shadow daunting, his gaze locked onto the children.

"Henry?" Faith's voice squeaked as she poked her head around him like a mouse peeking from a hole in a wall. To her, the man looked like a giant. "Why is he just standing there?"

Henry's fingers twitched as his mind searched for the grown-up thing to do—*He ain't threatened us or tried ta take our stuff...maybe he's waitin' fer others ta help him out? I know what Pa'd have done...stepped right up ta the man an' yelled in his face ta "mind yer own damn business." Gid coulda fought 'im, but he ain't done nothin' but stand there. Words then. Maybe I can talk him away.*

When Henry finally spoke, his voice cracked before settling into his regular tone. "Ya know when the next train comes through, mister?"

"Mo," the man said, his deep voice resonating like the toll of a church bell.

Henry cocked his head, confused by the man's reply.

The man's eyes flicked away from Henry's, glancing past him before shooting back. "Mo," he said again, this time with a hint of enthusiasm.

Tiny fingers pressed against Henry's waist, his sisters growing more uncomfortable by the second. Slipping his hands to his hips, he gently squeezed his sisters' hands and nudged them down.

"What's he saying?" Grace whispered.

From the far side of the loading dock, an agitated voice called out, its nasal, high-pitched shrillness ear piercing. "Git yer big butt back here this instant. They ain't ready fer ya yet, Mo!"

Looking down at the children, the man smiled. His stubbly chin lifted in a grin, his lambchop sideburns framing his wide face. He glanced over his shoulder, and, in that motion, his face caught just enough light to reveal eyes as innocent as those of the children. When he looked back, his smile seemed to stretch from ear to ear.

"Mo," he said a third time, patting his chest, then spun around and marched away, arms swinging and boots tromping across the wood deck. Both relief and understanding washed over Henry. As he watched the large man walk off, he caught sight of his mother exiting the ticket office. She waved, lifting their tickets as if to show them, then pointed toward town. She mouthed words, then turned and stepped away from the depot.

"Look," Faith said, pointing. "Where's Mama going?" She started to follow when Henry pulled her back by the collar.

"Hey," she protested.

"Ma's got somethin' ta do that don't concern us kids. She'll be back soon enough."

"I'm hungry," Grace said, clutching her stomach.

Henry sighed, feeling the weight of his younger, needy sisters beginning to nag at him. "Why don't y'all look in one of the bags. I think there's some wrapped bread, maybe some jerky. That'll hold ya over 'til Ma gets back."

While the girls foraged through the bags for something to eat, Henry sat on the edge of the loading dock with his feet dangling over the side. He kept watch— half his attention on town, waiting for his mother, the other half on the big guy called Mo.

It was still early, but the streets were slowly waking as businesses opened their doors and proprietors arranged their wares along the boardwalk. A few stragglers appeared from the Star Hotel. They walked on stiff legs toward Blueberry Mike's Saloon and Eatery, a common place for morning respite with fixes for the hungry or the hungover. He shifted his gaze to the jail, then to the sheriff's office door. No sign of his mother yet.

Further down the street, Henry spotted the preacher now standing in front of the church steps. Respected for his godly ways and peaceful demeanor, the preacher made a point of being seen on early mornings when the local dregs and shameful sinners attempted to escape the clutches of the previous night's engagements. Whether it was overindulgence or moral depravity, men and women alike would inevitably crawl from the cracks, and the preacher was always there, watching as they slinked home. He would tap his Bible against his leg, lifting his hand in silent prayer for their souls— never judging, only watching. Henry recalled the preacher's words from months ago.

"Judge not, that ye be not judged. For with what judgment ye judge, ye shall be judged: and with what measure ye mete, it shall be measured to you again. Matthew chapter seven, verses one and two. Do you know what that means, young Henry?" the preacher had once asked him.

Henry had shrugged, having no idea. At his father's behest, the Morgans were not regular churchgoers, but they were well known around town, not always for the right reasons, thanks to Cletus.

"It means," the preacher had explained, "it is better to do right by yourself so that when your time comes to face the Almighty, His judgment of you will not be clouded by your own unjust scrutiny of others."

In the distance, the faint sigh of a train whistle drifted in with the breeze. A hum along the tracks preceded the train like waves parting before the bow of a ship. A moment later, it sounded more distinct, its high-pitched blast announcing its arrival to town.

Henry turned as Mo dashed to the edge of the tracks, pointing with childlike excitement, his body wobbling on fidgety feet. The ticket agent popped out of his office and joined Mo. To Henry's surprise, he patted Mo on the shoulders, his steadying touch helping to corral the big man's excitement as they shared a quiet moment watching the approaching train. When the ticket agent finally spoke, Mo looked down at him with the same admiration he held for the train, then leaned in to listen. After a moment, Mo nodded and glanced at the children.

As the ticket agent returned to his office, Mo strode back toward Henry and the girls, his crisp smile widening with each new blast of the train whistle as it rumbled closer to the station.

"Henry," a voice shouted from a distance.

"Look," Grace shouted. "It's Mama."

Turning, Henry saw his mother walking toward the depot, her pace swift and determined. He stood up, and climbed onto the driver's bench, preparing for his next job—sell the wagon. Liza did not call out again. Her feet carried her forward, just shy of running. The closer she got, the more Henry sensed something was wrong.

Behind him, a deep voice rang out. "Mo."

Henry turned to find the big man standing near their belongings. The girls, no longer afraid, did not shy away this time. Instead, they giggled at his enthusiasm and sudden reaction as the train blew its whistle again. He posed no threat, so Henry returned to watching his mother.

Liza closed the distance and spoke as she climbed a small wooden ladder onto the loading dock beside the wagon.

"Go, Henry. Quickly. The train will only be here a short time. Sell the wagon and the horse and get back here as fast as you can."

"The horse, too?" Henry's stomach dropped. "I thought—"

"The cost was too much, Henry. I'm sorry, but the horse must go with the wagon."

Henry's chest tightened. "But—"

"We do not have time to discuss it further. We'll be

lucky enough to get anything at all this early and with little to no time. I'll stay with your sisters." She glanced at Mo leaning over, hands on knees, and smiling at the girls. "I see you've met the porter."

Henry frowned. The harsh reality of his responsibility weighed on him, but he could not let his mother down. Not after everything they had gone through in the past twenty-four hours.

"Fine," he muttered. He wanted to argue, to insist they keep the horse, but there was no room for debate. Not now.

Liza stepped to the edge of the loading dock, reached into her pocket, and pulled out a ticket, handing it to Henry. The rhythmic chuff-chuff-chuff of steam pistons filled the brief silence left by the erratic wail of the train's whistle.

A heavy, sooty scent of burning coal drifted ahead of the train, carried by the wind. Interwoven with it was a faint metallic tang and the warm scent of hot iron, the taste settling on Henry's tongue as he inhaled.

Liza started to speak, but another shrill whistle blast swallowed her words. Exasperation twisted her face, impatience plain in her eyes.

"Meet us at the seats. Everything should be on the train before you get back."

Henry took the ticket and slipped it into his pocket. Grabbing the reins, he released the brake, but before heading out, he turned back to his mother. "Is everything okay?" he asked.

She stole a glance toward town, her fingers tightening briefly around her skirt before forcing a smile. "Yes, Henry. Everything is fine. Run along. Do your job."

"Yes, ma'am," Henry replied. He wanted to believe

her, but he was sure she was holding something back. He faced forward, noting his horse's ears flicking in anticipation. With a final glance toward his mother, he gave the command. "Walk on."

CHAPTER TWENTY-EIGHT

WILL AND GID LED THEIR HORSES THROUGH PATCHES OF rugged terrain, untouched by regular travel. The ground bore the faint imprints of horseshoes, subtle signs left by the riders they pursued. Every scuffed patch of dirt, every broken twig, every uneven indentation in the earth told a story, one they were determined to follow.

As morning spread, yellow beams cast pink and orange glows across distant rock faces, while the sounds of the West stirred to life on the lonesome prairie. Soaring overhead, a red-tailed hawk gracefully glided, its sharp eyes scanning the ground below for small prey. A family of jackrabbits darted about in search of morning silflay, their noses twitching at the scent of dew-dropped grasses nearby. Prairie dogs' heads bobbed up and down from darkened burrows, their black eyes and chattering teeth on the lookout for predators that might threaten their colony. And a herd of mule deer grazed together, ears twitching, tails wagging, guarded by a watchful buck, the monarch of the range, its dominance on constant display.

Wind whistled through mesquite, rattling the brittle branches, and brushed past Will and Gid as they continued west.

"Ya see all that?" Gid said, waving a hand, tracing the distant horizon with his finger. "We been all over, but it's hard ta beat the beauty of the rugged West."

Will nodded, breathing deep, filling his lungs with fresh air. "A-yuh. Mornings like this make a man want to disappear into nature. Hunt a little. Fish a little. Maybe kick his heels up next to a campfire and watch the land turn into a mystery after the sun goes down."

"Ever think we'll settle inta a place, Will?" Gid asked.

Will leaned to the side and spat. "Maybe. Maybe not. But I know this, once we do, there's no telling what we'd be missing over the next rise. Hell, we still haven't seen the Pacific. For that one reason alone, I don't see us planting roots any time soon."

"Guess yer right about that." Gid squinted his eyes, picking out another clue in the dirt, confirming they were still headed in the right direction. "Ya know, these two ain't so smart."

"How you figure?" Will asked.

"I'm thinkin' that if they were cold-blooded killers, they wouldn't be ridin' too far from the main trails. Men like that are usually smart. Stray too far off inta the wild, ain't no one around, which is kinda good, but also, ain't no one ta steal from, which'd be bad. Reckon these two are lettin' the horses do the thinkin'. And what with all the prairie dog towns, it's a might dangerous. One wrong move an' *SNAP*, yer stranded by a horse with a broken leg."

"Ya ain't wrong, Gid. Also, means we ought to be

extra careful." Glancing ahead, Will pointed out a strip of green in the distance. "Let's see if the tracks lead in that direction. With all that growth, there's bound to be some water. Possibly a stream or a river. The horses could use a good drink. That'll keep us from having to share our supply right away."

Gid nodded, patting the side of his horse. "Ya hear that? Might be yer lucky day."

The horse's ears swiveled, hearing a familiar voice and feeling his gentle touch. It bobbed its head as if agreeing with Gid, causing Will's horse to do the same.

"Don't look now, but I think that mighta given them a spark. Race ya, brother?"

Will looked around, surveyed the terrain, and shook his head. "It'd be crazy to chance an injury way out here."

"Afraid ya gonna lose? Again?" Gid said, the challenge of sarcasm in his voice.

Will laughed. "Gid, I can't remember the last time you beat me in a race."

"That's on account of yer older and forgetful."

"That so?" Will said, a sly grin curling the corner of his mouth.

"It is," Gid replied.

Will tightened his grip on the reins, waiting for just the right moment. "You know, Gid," Will started to say.

Gid turned his head. "What's that?"

The second Gid took his eyes off the path, Will dug in his heels and shot forward, his horse bursting into a gallop.

"That son of a gun," Gid muttered. He squeezed his legs tighter around his horse, loosed the reins, and hollered, "Hee-yaw!"

CHAPTER TWENTY-NINE

MAIN STREET STRETCHED BEFORE HENRY, SEEMING TO grow longer and narrower as he drove the wagon and his horse toward the blacksmith. Located two buildings past Blueberry Mike's and the sheriff's office, it should have been a short ride, but it felt as if Henry were driving toward the edge of the world.

Sell the wagon, that was our deal. Not the horse...not the horse.

Henry's throat began to burn. His nose ran. A glimpse of childhood normalcy fought its way into his mind, threatening to pull him back to the boy he once was—before everything changed.

It's not fair.

Lost in thought, Henry rocked with the wagon's jolts, its suspension groaning for fresh lubrication.

In a daze, Henry caught a flicker of movement out of the corner of his eye. Sheriff Wolfe stood on the board-walk in front of the jail, watching him. His eyes were slits tucked beneath the shadowed brim of his hat. He followed Henry with a gaze more suited for a guilty man than a boy, but stare at him he did, swiveling at the waist as the wagon rolled past. After a moment, Wolfe stepped off the planks and disappeared inside the sheriff's office.

Henry's trusted horse carried him forward, its head bobbing in rhythm with each step.

The scent of fresh pastries and sizzling bacon wafted from Blueberry Mike's, teasing Henry's empty stomach. It was already tied up in knots over what he was tasked with doing, and the tempting smells only exacerbated his mounting discomfort.

Could today get any worse?

He watched his horse's head bob back and forth, its ears pricked forward, ready to flick at the first unexpected sound.

Ahead, the blacksmith's shop stood at the edge of the boardwalk, its roof overhang sheltering a clutter of tools, horseshoes, and iron scraps that dangled from hooks.

The closer Henry drew, the sharper the scent of hot iron and burned coal became, tinged with the faintest trace of oil. The blacksmith had not yet noticed him, too focused on his morning ritual of setting up shop. Henry gripped the reins tighter. The blacksmith might not care about his business today—but Henry sure did.

Pulling to a stop, the horse and wagon blocked the entrance to the shop. Henry set the brake and looped the reins around the lever. His hands prickled as numbness crawled through his fingers. Balling his hands into fists, he took a deep breath and hopped down from the bench.

The blacksmith, John Amos, was already at work. A burly man in a soot-streaked apron, he hefted a small wooden keg from a shelf and carried it toward the forge. Setting it down with a heavy thud, he yanked the stopper free and tipped it forward, pouring a stream of water into the quenching trough. A hiss of steam curled into the air as the liquid met lingering embers from the night before.

Henry watched as the man wiped his brow with the back of his wrist, then rolled the keg aside with a practiced shove. His thick arms flexed as he reached up, adjusting a row of hanging tools—long-handled tongs, heavy hammers, and coiled lengths of chain swaying slightly in the morning breeze.

"Mr. Amos." Henry's voice was low, barely audible.

Don't be scared, Henry.

"Ain't the place ta be leavin' a wagon, boy."

The blacksmith continued setting up shop. Henry spoke again, this time more confident and with a tone more forceful than he intended. "Mr. Amos. I come ta sell ya the wagon"—he turned to glance at his horse, its deep, dark eyes admiring him back. He swallowed hard before adding—"and the horse."

"Nope, don't need a cart er horse. Got my own."

Henry stepped into the dense maze of iron tools and metal fashions, feeling the heat from the forge press against his cheeks.

"I'm only lookin' ta fetch a fair price, Mr. Amos. Say, forty dollars? That ain't much."

The blacksmith laughed to himself. "Forty dollars?" He paused for a moment and looked past Henry. "Son, even if I was needin' a wagon, I wouldn't go wastin' money on that one."

A chill ran through Henry. Unsure of what to do, he blurted out the first thing that came to mind. "What about fer parts? There's lots of good iron ta salvage? An' the wood? It's mostly sturdy. If ya ask me, Mr. Amos, I'm offerin' ya a bargain."

The blacksmith picked up a cloth and wiped his hands, then tossed it onto a barrel filled with nails. He walked over to Henry, his mass towering before the boy.

"I know you. I've seen ya around town. Yer Cletus Morgan's kid."

Henry pressed his lips together and nodded.

"Buster, right?" Amos said, staring down at him. "Yer pa sendin' ya ta do his business now, boy?"

"No sir," Henry replied. "Pa was killed last night. Shot dead on the way home."

Amos stiffened. His jaw twitched, but he said nothing. Instead, he scratched the back of his neck.

"I need the money ta help git my family ta Amarillo," Henry continued. "They're waitin' at the depot right now."

Brushing past Henry, the blacksmith walked over to the wagon. Henry followed, watching as the man inspected it. Amos moved around the wagon, slow and steady, running his hand over the hubs, pressing his boot against a rear wheel to test its give. When he grabbed the side wall and rattled it, the wood groaned, one board splintering beneath his grip. He clicked his tongue and shook his head, then worked his way to the front, patting the horse on the neck when it turned to look at him. Seeing Henry watching his every move, Amos noticed the pain behind his eyes.

"I gotta be honest with ya, Buster."

Before he could stop himself, Henry interrupted. "It's Henry, now, Mr. Amos."

"Okay, Henry," Amos chuckled as he walked over to

rejoin him. "Here's what I'm willin' ta do. It's like I said, I ain't needin' a wagon or a horse…"

Henry's shoulders slumped.

"But," Amos said, his voice rising enough to offer Henry a bit of hope. "I'll give ya twenty dollars fer the wagon, but I just can't take the horse."

He turned and waved to his shop, its wares filling every square inch of the establishment. "I ain't got no room fer a horse. Maybe try the livery. If ya run into a dead end or yer outta time, there's always the knackers."

Henry's blood ran cold at the thought of selling his horse at all, but the mention of knackers was an icicle through the heart. Amos walked into his shop, pulled a small wooden box from a shelf on a rear table, and opened it. Henry watched as he removed a handful of bills and made his way back through the maze of iron-works ready for sale and stuck the wad out for him. "Here. Take it. I'll unhitch yer horse an' have it tied out front an' ready fer when ya sell it."

It was not a lot of money, but it was better than nothing. Henry took the bills and stuffed them in his pocket. "Thank you, Mr. Amos."

The blacksmith nodded, then walked to the wagon and began the chore of unbuckling the straps and loosening the traces.

From across town, Henry heard the blast of the train whistle. Its shrill warning was a kick to Henry's backside that he did not have much time to complete his tasks. *"Sell the wagon and the horse,"* his mother had said.

He exited the blacksmith shop and headed for the livery, praying he would not have to consider the alternative.

The Clarendon Livery was run by Edgar Hunt, an

older man whose family had owned and operated the business as long as Henry could remember. Centrally located, it was the ideal spot for travelers and locals alike. While Hunt was a businessman, he also knew the value of relationships, some he maintained to elevate his standing among the influential of town.

For years, he had provided the mayor and whoever was sheriff at the time a reliable place to keep their horses, free of charge, so long as they looked out for his interests should any issues arise. It was an unspoken quid pro quo, not unknown to the townsfolk, but only acknowledged in whispers or after too many shots of whiskey led to an unintended slip of the lip. Hunt also benefited from information overheard in the shadows of the stalls—the careless words of men unaware the walls had ears and the faint whispers of those who knew they did.

Henry walked to the edge of the livery and peered through the wide doorway, taking in the rows of stalls beyond. The scent of fresh manure and stale hay filled his nose. To his left, neatly stacked bales lined the near wall. In front of him, stalls stretched throughout the barn, most of them empty, though the soft shuffle of hooves and low murmurs of animals echoed from deeper within.

Lifting his chin, he started to call out, but at the last moment, he smothered the words when angry voices burst into the barn to his right. The sudden noise made him jump. Instinct kicked in, just as it had many times before when his pa came home drunk, busted out from faro, or both. Quick as a barn rat caught in the open, he scurried behind the pyramid of hay.

"God damn it. Git the horses saddled and ready."

"What happened?"

Henry listened, recognizing the first voice from the start. Sheriff Wolfe. The second he was less sure about, but he did not have to wonder for long.

"Hunt, ya know how we sent them men out ta the Morgan place last night to collect from the widow?" Wolfe's voice sounded tense. "Well, the widow just showed up at my office to report that each an' every one of 'em are lyin' dead outside her cabin. Them damn Crockett boys were still there an' killed the lot of 'em."

"Jesus. Did she know it was you who sent them?" Hunt's voice waivered, plunging into total nervousness.

Henry peeked between the bales, watching and listening.

"Didn't seem so," Wolfe said, pacing. "Now I gotta ride out there and see fer myself."

"And if it's true? I mean, Granger and his bunch were as tough as they come." Hunt said, his body twisting to follow the sheriff's movements.

Sheriff Wolfe stopped and glared at Hunt. "Ya can't be tough an' dead at the same time."

Hunt absorbed the heat with an uneasy step back. "What will you do?"

"If'n those men are dead like she said, I'm gonna bring the whole world down around the ones who killed 'em. There won't be a safe place in Texas fer them Crockett boys ta hide."

Henry's eyes grew large. His heart pounded his chest.

Gid and Will didn't do a thing except protect me and Ma. What was the sheriff saying...that they are killers?

"Get word to the undertaker, as well," Wolfe continued. "I gotta clean this mess up right before things get sticky."

"What about the widow? What hand does Liza have to play in this?"

"Hunt, if'n we can't catch the Crockett boys, we'll track down the woman in Amarillo. Haul her back here an' charge her fer the killings instead."

"Why Amarillo?" Hunt asked.

The sheriff turned to face the exit as the train's whistle screamed through town again. "'Cause that's where she an' her kids are headed right now. They're on the train."

Henry saw the evil scowl cut across the sheriff's face.

Ya ain't no lawman, Henry thought. *Yer a wolf in sheep's clothin'.*

Time ticked away, the seconds seeming to vanish like errant bullets shot into the sky. Henry's mind raced—*Gid and Will were in danger. The sheriff and his men would be after them for sure once they saw the scene at the cabin.*

Another long, shrill blast came from the depot.

As long as Ma and sisters stayed on the train, they were safe, for now.

"Git movin', Hunt." the sheriff's voice bellowed, reclaiming Henry's attention. "I want those horses ready as soon as my men arrive."

Henry watched Hunt shuffle away from Wolfe, disappearing down the long row of stalls on the far side of the barn. Wolfe lingered, as if sensing he was being watched.

After a beat, he stepped forward, approaching the fresh hay until he was close enough to lift a foot and rest it on the bottom bale. Leaning in, he plucked a single straw from the pile and stuck it in his mouth, chewing the end like a dead cigarette.

Henry did not move a muscle. The only sign of life was the subtle rise and fall of his chest, barely perceptible in plain view. He kept his breaths shallow, unnoticed by Wolfe.

Time trickled away, precious seconds Henry would never get back, but he was trapped, forced to wait, to do nothing until the sheriff left the livery. Then, a new voice cut through the quiet. Familiar from the night before, one of the deputies who argued with Gid on the way to find the killers' camp. "Sheriff."

Wolfe turned around. "Withers. Come with me. We've got work ta do."

Withers followed Wolfe away from the hay, disappearing down the same side of the barn where Hunt had gone.

Henry wasted no time. He shot out from his hiding place and sprinted at top speed. Skidding to a sudden stop onto Main Street, Henry looked to the train depot. Steam billowed from the locomotive. A few passengers waved from the train windows. If Henry did not get moving, he would miss the train. Looking over his shoulder, he spotted his horse tied in front of the blacksmith's shop.

Three short bursts from the train whistle signaled it was preparing to leave the station. Sweat beaded on Henry's brow. He gritted his teeth and took off running again just as a man's voice echoed from the depot. "All aboard!"

CHAPTER THIRTY

ONLY A MOTHER KNOWS THE DEEP, ANXIOUS ACHE OF A missing child—the long-held breath, the pounding palpitations, the pure terror stirred by helplessness, an anguish no scale in creation could ever measure.

Henry had one job to complete before returning to the depot to meet Liza and the girls for the ride to Amarillo. But as Liza peered out the passenger car window, her eyes darting from face-to-face in the growing crowd along Main Street, the realization closed around her like a tightening noose. He was not there. Three blasts of the train whistle. The conductor's final call, *"All aboard!"* A grim warning. The train was leaving, and Henry was nowhere to be seen.

Liza's gaze flicked to her daughters. Faith and Grace sat beside her, whispering, giggling, delighting in their first train ride, blissfully unaware of their mother's mounting distress. There was no leaving them to search for Henry.

She swallowed, but her mouth was dry. The meeting with the sheriff had only added to her unease, feeling more like a confession than a report. The nightmare from the night before resurfaced, continuing where it left off, but this time unraveling in real-time. Cletus was dead. Their home was lost. And now, in the firestorm of their escape, Henry was missing.

The windowpane felt cool against her palms as she pressed her hands to the glass, willing him to appear before it was too late.

Then, a sudden jolt. The locomotive lurched forward, couplings clattering like a row of falling dominoes.

No.

Liza shot to her feet, flung open the window, and leaned out, heedless of anything but her son.

"Henry!" Her voice, raw with urgency and fear, carried over the din of the station, drawing startled stares from bystanders. Let them look. Let them think her mad. She did not care. She saw nothing, heard nothing, felt nothing but the terrifying absence of her boy.

But Henry did not appear.

There was no frantic burst through the doorway, no breathless explanation of why she was making such a fuss.

She scanned the street, the crowd. *Everywhere.*

He was not coming.

And the train was not waiting.

CHAPTER THIRTY-ONE

THE ROUGH TERRAIN GREW MORE TREACHEROUS AS SULLY and Tater pressed on, their road to retribution leading them northwest. Unfamiliar with the area, Sully's impatience to claim their payday clouded his judgment, and his sense of direction, blinding them to the fact that they were edging closer to the southern stretches of Palo Duro Canyon.

"Ya sure this is right, Sully?" Tater looked ahead, eyes narrowing as he searched for a familiar landmark. "Don't recall bein' this way before."

"I know'd which way ta go, Tater. Don't go guessin' me wrong again."

"I ain,t but—"

"But nothin', dummy. Look," Sully yanked the reins back, bringing his horse to a sudden stop. "The sun's there." He jabbed a finger toward the sky, then made a sweeping arc, landing it on their path ahead. "An' we're goin' thata way. North."

Sully glared at Tater. What brotherly love he had for

him was buried beneath fresh scars and addictive dams of adrenaline, waiting to break loose. He had but one thought on his mind—reclaim what was his.

"Now shut up an' follow along. An' keep yer eyes peeled. The sooner we sell that saddle, the sooner yer load'll lighten. That outta cheer ya up."

Tater followed two horse lengths behind, his mind cluttered with confusion and exhaustion, not to mention the growing loss of confidence in the man he followed. Sully and Tater never had much to speak of, but what they lacked in possessions they had always made up for in brotherhood. Now, in the hell that they had created, Sully seemed lost to vengeance and madness. His mind was slipping, though Tater prayed it was not gone for good.

Tater glanced up. The sun seemed to shrink and, at the same time, grow hotter with each pressing hour. He squinted, then turned his head westward. Scattered mesquite trees and tufts of juniper spread out as far as the eye could see. Nestled just beneath the horizon, a thin green line ran until cut off by desolate brown, as if whatever lay beyond had fallen off the edge of the earth.

Facing front, two things came into view. First, a thin trail of black smoke coiled into the sky, streaking the blue with dark, threadlike tendrils. As the smoke climbed, it fanned out, a spreading stain across the heavens.

The second, and more immediate danger, was the sheer drop ahead.

Tater's stomach tightened. The ground vanished just yards in front of them. The land fell away into a narrow canyon, its jagged walls plunging deep. Though its opening spanned no more than twenty feet across, the drop was enough to cripple a man, if not kill him outright.

"Whoa, Sully. Watch out!"

Tater's warning ripped Sully out of the daydream he was enjoying, saving him from riding right off the cliff.

"Oh, shit," Sully yelled, wrenching the reins hard, bringing his horse to an abrupt halt.

Tater pulled up next to him and peered over the edge. The thought of not warning Sully, of letting him fall, never crossed his mind. Instinct had been faster than reason. But now, as they both sat safely astride their horses, staring out at the cut earth, the idea flickered in Tater's mind.

If he'd fallen, you'd be free, one inner voice teased. *I ain't no killer, no matter what*, another pushed back.

Tater gave his head a shake to clear his thoughts. "Close call, Sully."

"Damn straight, close call. How 'bouts a little more heads-up next time?" Sully reined his horse around and began backtracking the trail, searching for a way around. Tater let out a sigh, his breath heavy with frustration and second thoughts, and stared into the chasm below. Jagged rocks, packed dirt, wicked brambles, and pointed sticks formed a gaping maw, like the open mouth of a prairie monster waiting to chew up and swallow its next unsuspecting victim.

"I can't," he whispered as the voices argued inside of him.

"Hurry it up, Tater." Sully's voice echoed along the canyon rim. "I see somethin' up ahead. This could be our lucky day."

Tater pulled away from the edge and urged his horse forward.

"Maybe," he muttered, watching Sully riding ahead. "But luck don't always pan out."

CHAPTER THIRTY-TWO

SUNLIGHT GLINTED OFF THE WATER, FLASHING WITH EACH curl and dip of the murky current.

"Looks like the tracks follow the gully washer south," Will said, crouching near the edge of the swift-moving runoff.

Gid leaned over, the leather saddle creaking under his weight. He scanned both directions along the swollen creek bed before fixing his gaze on the tracks Will studied. "A-yuh. No sense crossin' here, 'less they're dumber than dirt. Water's movin', an' I cain't see the bottom. I reckon they felt the same."

Will stood and wiped his brow. As the sun climbed higher, the heat rose with it, causing sweat to bead along the brim of his hat. "Once we cross and find their tracks on the other side, we'll have a better idea of how far we are behind them."

"Let's get movin' then, Will."

Will nodded, then leaned over and splashed water across his face before mounting his horse.

They followed the same set of tracks south along the

swollen creek until the bed widened, spreading the water over a broader area.

As the current thinned, the water grew shallower, revealing a smooth, rocky bottom where ripples danced over the stones. Beneath the clearing water, rocks of various colors gleamed, shining like polished marbles on a hardwood floor.

Will stopped, inspecting the ground where the dirt turned to mud. Gid continued on another twenty yards before sliding out of the saddle.

"Lookie here," Gid called out, holding a mud-stiffened hat above his head. "Could be one of theirs."

"Could be anybody's," Will replied. "Plus, ain't no way of telling. Remember, Henry only heard the men's voices. He didn't see what they looked like or what they were wearing."

Gid climbed back onto his horse with the hat in hand and rode upstream to Will. "True, but maybe it's the piece of the puzzle we'll need ta confirm their identity once we catch 'em. If the shoe fits, ya know the sayin'."

"I know it," Will said, nodding. "Pack it away, and we'll hold onto it for now."

Gid stuffed the hat into his saddlebag for safe-keeping and led his horse to the water for a drink.

"Tracks enter the water here. Let's spread out," Will said. "Head back to where you found the hat and cross there. We can work our way back to one another once we've crossed to the other side. Holler if you find the trail again."

"Got it," Gid said, reining his horse around and guiding it toward his crossing point.

Even though the water was shallow, Will let the

horse adjust its pace. With the constant flow, there were no signs of anyone or anything having passed through the stream aside from the tracks they followed.

As expected, they had found deer and hog tracks along the water's edge, along with the occasional big cat print. The latter was unsettling but not surprising, making Will and Gid all the more watchful as they tracked the killers south. But underwater, nothing stayed in one place for very long, even in the gentlest flows.

Will eyed the shore. Gid kept his head down, watching the ebb and flow of the water swirling around the stones. Without warning, he hopped out of the saddle, landing with a jarring splash, then plunged his hand into the water at his feet.

"Gid. Hey! You, okay?"

Will pulled up and watched his brother fumble around in the water like he was bare-hand fishing. After a moment hunched over, Gid straightened, something clutched in his hand.

"Oh, yeah, Will. Had to jump in ta fetch somethin' from the bottom."

Not wanting to lose his position, Will stayed put and called out. "I hope it was worth the cost of riding wet."

Gid studied the object in his palm, then raised it over his head, a wide grin spreading across his face. "Arrowhead," he said. "Perfect condition." He tossed it into the air, caught it with ease, celebrating the find, then slid it into his saddlebag with the found hat, and mounted up. Dripping with pride, and from splashing about, he navigated a route to the opposite side of the stream and resumed his search for the killer's horse's tracks.

Will and Gid were both experienced trackers, honing their skills over a lifetime of hunting game and sometimes men. It was a craft to them, second nature, along with many other skills they had at their disposal. Before Gid's horse planted two shoes on dry earth, Will motioned him over, having already found the trail.

"Got 'em," he said, sliding out of the saddle. Will made it a habit to closely study the prints he was hunting, especially when losing then regaining their markings. If by some chance another pair of riders passed through, it would take a good deal of observation and recall to identify the correct tracks to follow. "I'd say we're about eight to nine hours behind."

He pointed to the markings in the dirt, then followed them until they disappeared into the water. "See? The prints nearest the water are still moist, but at the bottom of the indentation, there's a hint of drying. The coloring is different than on the surface. These farther away"—he pointed beyond the water's reach—"have dried more quickly, the ground having only been made wet by their saturated legs dripping down to their hooves."

"I'd agree with that, Will. We've got daylight on our side, so let's pick up the pace. Maybe we can shave some time off their lead."

The Crockett brothers continued a southwesterly trek, following tracks that looked as fresh as the moment they were made. With no bad weather rolling in to mask their way and only a gentle breeze that teased a coolness swirling within the rising heat, they increased to a trot, moving faster at times when the terrain allowed.

They pressed on, the land around them growing

sparse, even the hardy mesquites giving way to open ground. Will squinted into the distance, scanning the horizon—then, something caught his eye. He raised a hand signaling Gid to stop, then pointed to a spot in the distance. Slowing their horses to a standstill, Will pulled a spyglass from his saddlebag, extended it, and placed it over his eye.

"Whatcha see, Will?"

"Camp. Looks deserted." Will swept back and forth until one thing caught his attention. He lowered the glass and handed it to Gid. "Have a look."

Gid closed his left eye and peered through the pocket telescope with his right. He lowered it to take in the scene from afar, then replaced the glass and spoke while looking. "Hate ta say it, but it looks like we're headed in the right direction."

"So, you see it, then?"

"A-yuh." Gid lowered the spyglass and shared a look with Will. "'Nother body," he muttered.

"Stay sharp. It's doubtful the killers are still around, but let's not get caught with our pants down."

Gid collapsed the telescope and handed it to Will. "When have ya ever known me ta get caught with my britches down?"

Will smirked, but bit back his reply. Instead, he returned his gaze to the distant camp, eyes narrowing. "Come on, Gid. Let's ride in for a closer look."

They nudged their horses forward, closing the distance at a steady lope. As they neared, it was not the smell that confirmed what they had seen, but a cluster of flies swarming over the dead body.

Gid wrinkled his nose. "Ain't fresh, but it ain't old, either."

Will nodded. "A day at most."

They reined in a short distance from the camp, scanning for any sign of movement. The body lay sprawled, face down. Blood had dried dark beneath him, blackening his clothes in a mix of death and dirt.

Will dismounted first, his boots crunching against the dry earth. Gid followed, one hand resting lightly on the butt of his pistol. The fire pit was cold, just a shallow bed of white ash ringed by scattered embers. Boot prints littered the camp, more than one man could make alone. Gid surveyed their surrounds while Will approached the body.

Squatting beside the corpse, Will pushed his hat back, eyes narrowing as he studied the scene. "Shot three times," he murmured. He reached out and rolled the man over, revealing his mortal wounds.

"Close range," Will said, shaking his head.

Frozen in place, the man's mouth was agape. Grime clung to his lips like frosting on a cake. One eye was covered, mudded over, crusted with secretions and earth.

Gid exhaled through his nose. "Somebody wanted him dead. Got the drop on 'im."

Will scanned the ground, taking in the scuff marks, the kicked-up dirt, the way the body had fallen. "Strange."

"How ya figure?"

"The body's there," Will said, gesturing to the corpse. "But there's blood stains behind him as well as beneath. It's like they moved him after he'd been dead for a spell."

"Why the hell would they do that? Harder ta rifle a man's pockets when they're facin' the ground."

Gid crouched down beside Will. "These men we're after, seems like they ain't yer regular bandits. Seems like they're not operatin' with a full deck."

Will stood up. "Or new to the game. Either way, they're dangerous. All the more reason to catch 'em quick before they kill again."

Gid rubbed at his chin, glancing around the deserted camp. His eyes trailed off, catching something in the distance. "Well, what do ya know about that. Looks like the killers didn't make out with everythin'."

Will followed Gid's gaze.

"Bet ya a cold beer and a piece of pie that's his horse runnin' free over yonder," Gid said.

Will nodded. "See if you can wrangle in the horse. I'll look around and see if there's anything here that might tell us who the man was."

"We gonna bury 'im, Will."

"It'll take time, but it'd be the right thing to do."

Gid nodded in agreement.

"Let's work fast. Sun's burnin' high, and we've got ground to cover."

Gid mounted up in pursuit of the stray horse. Will knelt again and carefully searched through the man's pockets, his fingers brushing over a folded scrap of paper. He pulled it free, unfolding it with a frown.

It was an old photograph of a woman. Even with the creases in the paper, her natural beauty shone through. Turning it over, he found writing on the back. The ink had smudged, but the few words were still legible.

He read it once, then again, jaw tightening.

To my love, Hank, with whom only death may part us.

CHAPTER THIRTY-THREE

SULLY AND TATER WORKED THEIR WAY AROUND THE SMALL canyon, curling around the eastern rim and heading straight toward the source of the stringy smoke.

"When we git ta where's we're goin', ya let me do all the talkin', Tater."

"Ya ain't gonna shoot nobody, are ya? Two in as many days already ain't so good, Sully."

Tater waited for a reply, any acknowledgment that their jaunt into camp was not predicated on foul intent, but Sully's silence offered no reassurance. Killing had grown on Sully like mold on cheese. It ruined the good parts, burying the rest under a layer of rot that would have to be peeled away to find what was left, if anything remained at all. Continuing down this road was dangerous, and there was no end in sight.

As they approached the rising smoke, jagged drop-offs yawned wider, threatening to swallow them. Looking at the gaping rips in the earth stretching into the distance, they saw the land torn apart as if an ancient giant had dragged a pickaxe across the prairie, carving through rock and stone without regard.

"Look, Tater. I'm countin' three men. Ya see the same?" Sully said, his voice rough and gravelly.

Tater squinted, his eyes darting around the distant camp, landing on each man and confirming the number Sully had counted. "Yeah. Three, Sully."

"Okay. That ain't too many."

"But we're outnumbered," Tater said, his tone rising with concern.

"Don't go turnin' yella on me, Tater. We're just gonna see if'n they'll welcome us in. Tell us the best way ta Tascosa from here. Heck, maybe they'll even buy that saddle."

Sully's words sounded easy, but Tater did not buy it. He could feel the lie in his gut. Before he could reply, he saw his brother raise a hand and wave, hailing the men at the camp. "Howdy, friends," he called out, sounding to Tater like the friendlier man he once knew. "Ya have room fer a couple more?"

The men stood, watchful but unshaken by his call, but like any cowboy, they took precautions before giving an answer. One held a rifle by his side, a show of force without acting forceful. The other two shared a considering glance before the taller of the pair returned the wave, signaling the brothers forward.

"Nice an' easy, Tater," Sully said out of the corner of his mouth.

The two sauntered to the edge of the camp when the man holding the rifle moved it across his chest, cradling it. His eyes stayed fixed on the brothers, his face absent of expression. The taller cowboy was the first to speak.

"What brings ya out here, fellas?"

Sully opened his mouth, but Tater beat him to the punch. "Lookin' fer work. Was with the T-Diamond 'til a week ago."

"That so?" the tall man replied.

Sully grinned, presenting himself with a calm exterior, while inside, his thoughts were beating Tater to a pulp. "Yes, sir. Just like he said."

The man eyed Sully and Tater, his judgment looming over them like a lonely hangman's noose. Chills rippled down Tater's back as the silence between the man and his brother lingered. Finally, the tall man spoke again. "Refresh my memory, RJ Bryan still runnin' that spread?"

Sully hesitated, licking his lips before gritting his teeth, having no idea to whom the man was referring. He turned to Tater, fishing for an answer. "Bryan," he stammered, glaring at his brother.

"But it weren't RJ Bryan. That part's wrong," Tater said, deflecting the heat from Sully. "WJ Bryan's the title yer tryin' ta remember."

"That's right," the tall man said.

Tater should have stopped right there. His only requirement leading into the camp was to let Sully do the talking, but he could not even get that right. Instead, he gambled politeness and facts over-stretching the truth. "My name's Tater. This is Sully."

Had Sully been facing the front, the men would have seen the guilty twinkle in his eyes as they grew large on his face. Tater could see though, and knew by the snarling lips and chewing motions his brother made that he had just messed up. Sully swallowed hard, forced his face to relax, and turned back to the men. "An' who er y'all?" he said, straining to keep his cool.

The tall man answered for everyone. "I'm Bill Stanton." He gestured to the man next to him. "This is Earl Clack." Thumbing over his shoulder at the man holding the rifle, "That's Ben Reed. We all work fer Hank Wilson over at the Triple Bar S."

"Ain't never heard of that one," Tater said. "Any chance y'all er needin' some more men?"

Stanton turned to Clack, towering over him by more than six inches, and cocked his head. Clack stuck his fingers into the small pockets in his vest and rocked back on his heels, as if he held the power to make decisions.

"Why don't y'all slide on down an' join us by the fire," he said. "Discuss this over some coffee."

Tater was quicker than Sully again, answering for both of them. "An' how," he said, smiling. "We ain't had a good cup since—"

"Since we left the ranch," Sully said, cutting the sentence short.

Stanton laughed, his tall frame buckling. "He didn't say it was a good cup. Ol' Ben's in charge of cookin'. Yer more liable ta die from a taste of his brew than a rattlesnake bite, but it's all we've got, so we just smile and enjoy it, sip by sip."

Tater and Sully glanced at Reed, awaiting a retort, but his face remained stony. He did not laugh. He did not blink. He only shifted the rifle a little closer, a quiet reminder that coffee was not the only thing he knew how to handle.

Tater broke away from Reed's gaze and slid out of the saddle. "Sure feels good ta stretch a bit," he said. Swinging his arms back and forth, he stepped to the fire and took a seat on a large stone near the dancing flames.

Sully looked down on him, yet to dismount.

Don't git too cozy, brother.

Stanton retrieved a tin cup from a canvas bag resting near the gear pile opposite the fire ring. Clack squatted near the edge, stoking the glowing coals with a stick, but Reed was far less welcoming. "Ya gonna sit there all day, mister?" he said, his lips barely moving around the words.

Clack turned to Reed. "Easy now, Ben. These boys ain't a cause for you ta get all riled up." He then turned to Sully, his expression falling flat. "I ain't wrong, am I?"

Flicking his eyes away from Reed, Sully grinned, swung a leg over the saddle, and hopped down. "Shoot, Mr. Clack. Ya ain't wrong about nothin'." Sully stepped forward and extended his hand to him. "Just grateful fer a break an' a helpin' of the good stuff."

Stanton laughed again. Tater joined in, trying hard to garner acceptance among the men. Clack tossed the stick into the fire and shook with Sully. Reed stepped close, completing the circle of cowboys, but did not set the rifle aside.

"Help yerself," Reed said, lifting his chin to the steaming pot nestled on the coals. "I make it, but I ain't servin' it."

"Mighty kind of ya," Tater said.

He wasted no time kneeling and reaching for the simmering brew, his taste buds already salivating over the coffee he had not even tasted yet. As he reached for the handle, Stanton spoke up.

"Might wanna cover yer hand, lessin' ya don't mind gettin' burned. That pot's been on the fire a while now."

Tater flinched his hand away, pulled a bandana from his neck, and wrapped it around his fingers before gripping the handle. He chuckled at himself. "Got a little ahead of myself. Just smells so good."

Stanton shared a glance with Clack. Sully saw the questions in their eyes.

Yer diggin' yerself a hole, dummy.

As the men's gazes shifted back to Tater, Sully acted quickly to gain their attention instead. "Ya fellas know the way to Tascosa?"

His diversion worked, drawing all three of them to his question.

"Tascosa?" Clack said. "Thought y'all were lookin' for work?"

"Oh, we are," Tater said. "It's just..."

Sully's eyes flicked between Tater and Clack. His brother's mouth was leading them down a path he had not planned, and his patience was wearing thin.

"Just, what?" Clack asked.

"What Tater means is, we've got some business ta see about first," Sully explained. "He ain't wrong about the work part. Just jumpin' the gun again. If'n ya ever had empty pockets, ya know the feelin'."

"Been there," Stanton said, nodding.

Tater lifted his cup in thanks to their hosts, but before he took a sip, Sully spoke up, cutting him off. "Grab that extra saddle, Tater. Maybe one of them'll be interested or know someone who is."

The gleam in his brother's eye was commanding, a look he found uncomfortable, yet he did as he was told. Tater stood and placed his cup where he sat, then walked over to his horse. He could feel the men watching him as he unpacked the saddle.

"I ain't so sure we'd be interested in another saddle, friend," Reed said, circling around the fire to stand closer to Sully. "But I do like yer hat."

Reed could have used Sully's name. As a welcomed guest, he should have, but the blatant omission struck like a hot branding iron against his chest. He cocked his head, controlling the rising dislike of Reed, and swallowed his mounting discomfort. "I like it, too," he said, rolling his eyes to look up at the brim of the hat. "But, it ain't fer sale...*friend*."

Stanton raised his cup but paused, holding it at his lips. Caution crept into his gaze as he looked at Sully over the rim, the rising aroma lost to the thickening tension.

"No?" Reed replied. "Too bad. It reminds me of one a friend of mine wears."

Clack moved between them. "You tryin' ta stir up trouble with these men, Ben?"

"Oh, I ain't stirrin' nothin'," he said, eyes locked on Sully. "Tell me that hat don't look familiar and I'll let it go."

Clack faced Sully, studying the hat. After a moment, he glanced beyond him and saw Tater was walking back from his horse, lugging the saddle along.

"Well?" Reed said, his voice dripping with impatience.

Clack turned to his friend. "Damn, Ben. Sure, it looks like the boss's hat, feather an' all, but ya know how many just like it are out there?"

Stanton set his cup on the ground near the coals.

"He's got a point, Ben," he said. "But Earl, I was with Hank when he pulled a similar feather from an eagle we run across last spring. Fixed it smack dab in the leather hat band sayin' it was *too purty*, his words, to leave to the scavengers." His gaze turned to Sully. "Maybe our guest can tell us where he got it."

"I ain't got a problem with that," Sully said. "I got it—"

"Here it is," Tater interrupted, setting the saddle on the ground beside him. "Good leather. Tight stitchin'. Ain't a thing wrong with it 'cept we ain't need it." He looked up, all smiles, unaware that their presence in camp was now in question.

The men glanced at Tater, their eyes falling to the saddle at his feet.

"Well, I'll be a suck-egg-mule," Stanton said.

"What?" Tater replied.

Stanton walked around the fire to get a closer look at the saddle. Leaning over, he stroked the leather and ran his fingers along the saddle horn.

"Ya like it?" Tater asked.

"Like it?" Stanton said, all eyes engaged with him. "It's a beaut. But that there saddle belongs ta Hank Wilson."

"Who?" Tater said, still in the dark.

"He's sayin' it's their boss's, dummy. Prob'ly thinks ya stole it."

Stanton frowned at Tater. Tater looked back, confused by the sudden turn of events.

"I...I..."

Reed jerked his rifle to his shoulder and aimed the barrel at Tater, but Sully's newfound love of the kill saw him draw quicker, firing two bullets from his pistol. Reed never got a shot off. His chest buckled when the bullets struck. The first shot tore through his gut, exiting out the back. The other sliced into the meat of his chest, cracking bone, before lodging in his heart. He collapsed in a heap, his gun falling into the fire, knocking over the pot of hot coffee.

Time dragged and raced all at once.

Sully turned the gun on Clack, firing again and again. Each blast vibrated through him, the pleasure within surging. The blasts echoed, each seeming to clap louder than the last. Clack spun when the first bullet caught his shoulder. Had he immediately fallen, he may have had a chance. Instead, he fought to stay upright and absorbed the next shots in his side, then his neck. Falling to his knees, he clutched his throat, but there was no holding back the red river when the dam had broken. Blood spurted through his fingers, flowing down his neck. Earl Clack slumped to one side like a candle melting in the noonday sun.

Frozen in fear, Tater watched Sully empty his pistol into Clack. The dead, metallic *click* of the gun's hammer slamming into its empty iron frame was only a pause in the fight. Out of the corner of his eye, he saw Stanton turn and lunge for a rifle leaning against the pile of gear, but his gaze was held captive at the sight of the two dead cowboys. His mouth hung wide in disbelief.

Stanton moved fast for a tall man, grabbing and cocking the rifle with one fluid motion. Sully thrust his hand to his belt for fresh rounds. Whirling around, Stanton brought the rifle to his shoulder. With Sully in his sights and his finger on the trigger, his eyes narrowed.

Tater's eyes flicked to Sully.

He ain't lookin'!

CHAPTER THIRTY-FOUR

HOOVES POUNDED FORWARD, EACH STRIDE FOLLOWING fresh prints on a trail seeming to lead into the heart of Texas. Rolling plains dipped into flattened stretches of open prairie, scattered shrubs dotting the Llano Estacado. On a clear day, a man could see for miles in every direction, but with time running short and the path threatening to disappear, if not for a watchful eye following each elusive clue, losing focus for even a moment might mean losing the trail forever.

Blazing overhead, daylight burned at an alarming rate, and with the appearance of water swallowing what prints there were, it would take more than skill to recover. It would take a miracle.

CHAPTER THIRTY-FIVE

WILL AND GID STOOD OVER A FRESH MOUND MIXED WITH dirt and stone where they had buried the body of the beloved Hank. The creased photograph marked the head of the grave, pinned beneath four small rocks placed at each corner and sitting on a large stone pulled from the fire ring.

"Nothing more to do here," Will said, his eyes drifting to the north. "I figure we've got little less than half a day's light left before we lose the trail to darkness."

Gid knelt, scooping a handful of dirt from the top layer of soil, then let it sift through his fingers. Fine grains showered the grave like powdered sugar on a tart, but this was no sweet farewell.

"You gonna remember this place? We run across anyone who knew ol' Hank, they may wanna collect him."

Will nodded silently.

Gid stood and rubbed his hands together, the last of

the dirt wafting away and disappearing before it ever touched the ground.

Turning, Will and Gid were met by three pairs of eyes, large and curious, watching for their next move. The horses stood, ears pricked and listening. Hank's gelding had settled in with the other two but still seemed unsure about Will and Gid.

"Looks like our new friend is fittin' in just fine." Glancing back at the grave, Gid added, "It's a shame, though. It's a well-kept animal. A beaut." Looking up at the wide-open blue, he continued. "Don't ya worry, Hank. We'll do right by it, too, 'til we figure out where y'all came from."

Walking over to the horses, Will checked the saddle's cinch. Gid approached their refugee, admiring its coloring—large swirling patches of white speckled with auburn and coffee-colored spots running along its side and blending into three solid brown legs and one white foreleg. He reached out to stroke its two-tone muzzle. The horse bobbed its head at first, snorting a nervous warning, but kept its hooves planted.

"I know." Gid's gentle tone and slow approach calmed the animal. He placed his palm on its cheek, then ran his fingers down and around to its nose, then stroked its muzzle. Gid's horse whinnied, leaning close in search of a little love as well.

"Ya jealous?" Gid said. He placed his free hand on his horse and massaged its neck, working his way up to scratch between its ears. "See? I ain't lost on our new friend here. Just showin' him a little attention, that's all. Yer still my number one."

Will swung himself into the saddle. "As much as I

enjoy watching you flirt with the horses, might I remind you that we have some killers to catch?"

Gid was used to Will's sarcasm, and his point was made, but Gid could dish it just as good. He leaned close to his horse and kissed its nose. "Don't ya listen ta him. He's just sore in the saddle, that's all."

Gid shot Will a sideways glance and rolled his eyes before smiling, placing a boot in the stirrup, and climbing onto his horse's back.

They pulled away from camp together, Hank's pinto tied off to Gid's saddle, following alongside as they resumed their search.

The killers' trail out of the camp was easy to find, but the direction they had taken was puzzling.

"North?" Gid said. "Strange. Why the sudden change?"

"Dunno, but they've been unpredictable from the start. We've been lucky so far, having a clear path to follow. But with the direction they're headed, it won't be too long 'til they're in canyon country. The rocky terrain will hide their tracks."

"Yeah. An' if they decide ta hole up, we could be walkin' into an ambush," Gid added.

"Just keep a watchful eye," Will reminded. "They don't know we're hunting them. That alone favors us. But I don't expect a warm welcome when we do catch up."

The sky, void of clouds save for a peppering of buzzards circling in the distance, stretched in a vast royal blue, touching the horizon in all directions. The day was still, but not stale. Tufts of faint breeze brought unexpected relief, weaving through the sweat on the brothers' skin. It was not a scorcher, but with the sun reigning high above, there was no escaping its radiance.

The horses picked up speed, their strides lengthening as they settled into an easy lope. Will and Gid stayed focused, keen on the changes in the ground as the dust and dirt of the range hardened, signaling the transition to the rockier north.

The horses loped on, dust curling in their wake. Ahead, the land stretched wide and unforgiving. The killers had the lead, but Will and Gid felt it—they were catching up.

CHAPTER THIRTY-SIX

SMOKE SWIRLED FROM THE MOUTH OF THE BARREL. THE harsh scent of gunpowder hung heavy in the air, stinging the nose with its bitter stench. The sudden blast echoed into the canyon, ricocheting off its sheer cliffs as if reluctant to fade.

And then came the laughter, raw and wild, rising like a jackal hidden in the stony maze.

Tater's hands trembled as he lowered the gun, his last-second shot the only thing keeping Sully from being killed. His breath came shallow, his vision narrowing to a blackened tunnel where only one thing remained in focus—the agonized grimace of the man he had just shot.

Stanton staggered on spindly legs, his rifle slipping from his grasp as he clutched the bleeding hole in his side.

"Woo-ee!" Sully whooped, rushing over and chanting, "Hit 'im again."

Tater's jaw dropped. His cheeks sagged. The

smoking gun dangled at his side, its weight pulling at him with unbearable force.

Sully eyed Tater's dazed expression and slapped him on the back, hoping to snap him out of it. Instead, the jolt made Tater drop his gun.

"I...I...killed him." Tater's shock swallowed him whole.

Sully shot him a hard, questioning look, then turned to watch Stanton struggle with his injury.

"Nope, dummy. He ain't dead, yet." Sully bent over and picked up Tater's pistol. "Here. Finish the job."

Slapping the gun into Tater's empty hand, Sully lifted his brother's arm, forcing his fingers around the grip.

"There. Now, alls ya have ta do is point and shoot. Yer halfway there."

Tater's bottom lip quivered. Slowly, he turned his head, eyes wide, searching Sully's face. He tried to speak, tried to say, *I can't*, but all that came out was a jumbled, choking slur.

Sully frowned. "What? Ya sayin' ya can't, or ya won't?"

Stanton clawed at the dirt, dragging himself inch by inch toward the base of his camp's supplies. With a painful groan, he twisted and pushed himself upright, leaning against the pile, his breath coming in ragged gasps. He raised a hand in surrender, his palm shaking in front of him.

Blood beaded at the corner of his mouth. A wet, raspy sound bubbled in his throat.

"Do it," Sully growled.

Stanton's lips parted. "Don't. Just..." he croaked.

Something shifted inside Tater.

I ain't a killer.

Those words were all he needed to hear.

As his head cleared, disgust burned through his fear, stiffening his spine. His breath steadied. His hands no longer trembled.

Without a word, he pushed the gun into Sully, pulling his empty hand away.

Sully caught it before it hit the ground, his chest puffing as he sneered through gritted teeth. "Ya finally growin' a backbone?"

Tater shoved past him.

Sully stepped forward, grabbing for his arm. "Where ya goin'?"

Tater yanked free.

"Tater!" Sully's voice sharpened, turning to a growl. "I said, where ya goin'?"

Reaching his horse, Tater swung into the saddle, refusing to look back.

Sully's voice chased after him, lower this time. "I'm warnin' ya."

Tater finally turned—and froze. His breath hitched as he found himself staring down the muzzle of his own pistol.

Ya gonna shoot me, too, Sully?

"Git on down from there. We got things ta do before *we* leave, Tater."

Tater stiffened, his temporary bravery wearing thin.

"Go on," Sully continued, gesturing with the gun.

With mounting reluctance, Tater swung a leg over and hopped off the horse. Sully walked over, his eyes wild yet he moved with a calm more frightening than if he had lost his temper. Stopping close enough that Tater could smell his brother's breath, Sully took a moment to let his invasion of space settle in. Aside from the crackle of dwindling coals and the slowing rasp in Stanton's breathing, a quiet draped around them. Nearly nose to nose, Sully raised the gun, pressing the barrel against Tater's stomach.

Doubt flooded Tater, drowning out reason. For a fleeting second, death felt like the only escape. The thought should not have made sense, but in Sully's world, nothing did.

With a single fluid motion, Sully pulled back, flipped the gun in the air, caught it by the cooling barrel, and thrust it into Tater's chest, a near replay of how he just acquired it. "Here, Tater. Ya dropped this."

Losing the battle to subconscious reflexes, Tater's hands wrapped around the gun as Sully let go and stepped back. He swallowed then looked at the gun as if he held a dead opossum in his hands.

"Slip that inta yer holster an' help me straighten a few things up around here before we set out."

Biting his lip, he lowered his hands and slipped the gun into his holster, its weight heavier than it had ever felt before. His stomach churned as he avoided looking at Sully, the unspoken threat still lingering between them. He knew better than to argue. Knew better than to show weakness. As the moment stretched, the truth settled in—Sully was not giving him a choice.

Tater took a step foward, the back of his throat burned with everything he could not say.

Sully's gaze stayed on him, sharp and expectant. Seeing Tater comply brought a wolfish smile to his face. "See? That weren't so bad, was it?"

Sully stretched out a hand, a peaceful motion meant to ease the tension. Tater took it to shake but felt the immediate tightening of Sully's grip as he was yanked off balance. With ruthless precision, Sully landed a solid punch to Tater's gut.

The air shot from Tater's lungs in a strangled gasp. His knees buckled, his stomach twisting in violent protest. He crumpled, choking on the breath that would not come, his fingers clawing at the dirt like a man drowning on dry land. A warm mix of dust and gravel pressed into his cheek, grinding his skin as his mouth gaped, searching for air.

Sully loomed over him. He pressed a boot on Tater's hip and nudged him over to his back. Wheezing, Tater lay flat, his neck and face beet red as he strained for a full breath.

"Don't cross me, Tater. Bein' brothers is what's keepin' ya alive." Sully knelt next to him, his tone shifting. "Tell ya what. Kick back an' relax while I clean up. It'll do ya some good. Maybe give ya that extra energy we'll need once we reach Tascosa."

Tater nodded, the shock to his stomach still pulsating.

Sully stood and walked over to Ben Reed's dead body. He glanced at Stanton, his face blanched, drained of all color. Mocking Stanton's pain with an exaggerated grimace, Sully looked back at the corpse. "Mr. Stanton said ya were in charge of coffee. Ain't that somethin'? If only ya had poured me a cup, things mighta been differn't."

Sully leaned over and rummaged through Reed's pockets.

"Empty? Figures as much," he grunted grabbing him by the arms. Grumbling at the corpse, he began dragging him out of camp.

"What'er ya doin', Sully?" Tater asked, sitting up.

The scrape of Reed's body against the earth grated through the quiet, the harsh grind of gravel and small rocks crunching beneath his dead weight. The sound was as rough and unsettling as it looked.

"I told ya. Straightening things up 'round here."

Sully continued dragging Reed until they reached the rim of the canyon. He stopped and let go of Reed's arms, then faced Tater. "Hey. Ya 'member back ta when we was kids, an' Pa would try an' play with us down by the river?" Sully said.

A chill coursed through Tater's bones.

"What was that rhyme he'd always be sayin'?"

Sully wiped his brow with his palm, waiting for a reply. Tater opened his mouth to speak, but Sully interrupted. His face lit up. "I got it! Part of it anyhow."

Bending over, he grabbed Reed's arms again, swinging them back and forth like it was playtime, like he was a child.

Sully's voice took on a sing-song lilt, the same way their father once had, but twisted. "Dum dee dum, Fiddle dee dee...somethin', somethin' on my knee. Hold on tight, don't be slow, hang on now, and away we go!"

Sully's swings grew wilder, his cadence rising with the tempo.

Stanton made a strangled sound, half gasp, half plea. His eyes flicked to Tater, then back to Sully. He knew what was coming.

The last word left Sully's lips in a sharp exhale as he slung Reed's body over the ledge.

A long second stretched. Then, far below, a sickening, bone-snapping thud echoed up from the canyon floor.

Tater flinched, his stomach twisting. He could not stop himself from imagining the way Reed's body must have broken on the rocks, limbs bending in unnatural ways. His throat tightened, bile creeping up, but he swallowed it down.

Sully turned and punched at the sky, drunk on the moment, celebrating his ill-minded victory.

"Well, hell. That was fun." Sully exhaled, stretching his arms overhead like a man waking from a restful nap. Marching back to camp, he let out a triumphant whoop, his grin splitting too wide, his eyes burning too bright.

"Now...who's next?"

CHAPTER THIRTY-SEVEN

AS THE DAY PROGRESSED AND THE SUN DIPPED LOWER ON the horizon, lengthening shadows turned even the smallest objects into obstacles, masking the killers' ever-hardening trail. Each step forward demanded sharp eyes and unwavering focus, yet the spoor grew fainter, more elusive, complicating the hunt with every passing moment.

More than once, Will and Gid were forced to spread out, the trail vanishing in an instant. Each time, it led to frustrating delays, forcing them to slow their pace. As they reached a stretch of land that rolled like waves in the open ocean, they stopped to water their horses. Will wore a sour expression.

"At this rate, any ground we may have gained has probably been given back," he said.

"Ain't no tellin', Will," Gid replied. "One thing's fer sure, the killers make it to a ranch or town, anywheres with more than just the two of 'em, our search'll be over."

Will cast his gaze across the horizon. "Not much but Texas as far as the eye can see."

He stepped away from Gid, shading his eyes as he scanned the sky, then paused on a spot northwest of their position. At first, it was faint, almost imperceptible, but the longer he looked, the more certain he became. Walking to his horse, he reached into his saddlebag, retrieved his spyglass, and returned to the same spot. Raising the small telescope to his eye, careful to avoid the dipping sun, he swept across the distant sky and then down to the ground beneath. Lowering the glass, he narrowed his eyes and reassessed what he had seen.

"Gid. Come take a look."

Gid joined Will and took a turn looking through the glass.

"Tell me what you see," Will said.

Gid took a moment. With the spyglass still raised, he spoke.

"Fer starters, a lotta damn buzzards interested in somethin'." He paused, taking a step forward. "Strange, though. I see 'em circlin' and divin', but it's like they're divin' inta the ground. Prob'ly swoopin' inta a canyon, best I can tell."

"See anything else?"

Gid took another step forward. "Yeah. My eyes might be playin' tricks, but I swear I see a faint smoke trail. It ain't much. Like coals that rekindled on a piece of unburned wood." He lowered the spyglass. "If I had ta say, sure looks like a camp ta me. Think it could be them?"

"Only one way to find out," Will replied.

Gid handed the glass to Will as they walked back to the horses. Before mounting, Gid took in the scene behind them. The sky had begun to show its age. Its deep blue faded to pale purple just above the horizon. It was subtle, but an unmistakable sign that nightfall was coming. But that was not what caught his attention. Against the blending colors, something stirred—a faint brown smudge trapped in the waning blue.

Riders? he wondered.

The blur was too far away to tell if it was riders or a herd of deer racing across the terrain.

From the saddle, Will called out. "See something?"

Gid turned and swung himself onto his horse. "Nah. Maybe a dust trail. Wrong direction anyhow." He nudged his horse forward, the pinto falling in step beside them. "Ain't gonna worry about what's behind us. Only thing that matters is that-a-way." He pointed ahead.

Will nodded. "Let's move, then. With the rocky terrain and daylight at our backs, we'll have plenty of cover until we're close enough to see if it's a camp or something else."

They rode single file, Will taking the lead and guiding their way. As they closed the distance, the ground turned ragged, sheer drops appearing with little warning until a long, deep chasm to the west revealed itself. The vastness of its jagged depths swallowed the light, its rocky face catching the sun's lingering rays, deepening into shades of orange and red just below the canyon rim. The kettle of buzzards wheeled closer, their dark forms growing more distinct, their circling flight path shaped by the canyon's rising currents.

Riding up to the rim of a smaller canyon, the brothers stopped to discuss their next move. Remaining in the saddle, each studied the land before them and the behavior of the birds. The smoke they thought they had seen had disappeared, but they knew where they needed to go.

"What ya think, Will? Ride together or split up?"

Will leaned and spat, then took a swig from his water pouch before offering it to Gid. "I say we stay together. If it is our killers, we'll need to watch each other's backs. If it's someone else and we're split up, it may look like we are up to no good. Whoever we come across, we don't want to spook 'em."

"Agreed," Gid said.

They followed the edge of the canyon to a point where they could see what was left of a campsite, though its disheveled appearance told the brothers two very important things—the killers had been here, but Will and Gid were too late.

The firepit smoldered. Thin strings of white smoke swirled before vanishing into the air. Three horses remained tied to the low-hanging branch of a lonely mesquite. They gave a glance, ears pricking at the sounds and smells of strange men on strange horses, but remained indifferent and calm. Trash littered the ground, and discarded supplies left for scavengers lay strewn about.

"Hello to camp," Will called out, his senses on high alert.

When no one answered, Gid gave it a try. "Friendlys comin' in."

Still, no answer. Will and Gid shared a knowing look before proceeding to the center of the ramshackle camp.

"I'm gettin' tired of bein' one step behind, Will," Gid said as he dismounted. "I know we ain't been on the trail long, but fer everythin' we've come across, it feels like we've been travelin' fer days."

Will scanned the area, taking in their surroundings. "There," he said, pointing. "Blood trail."

Gid turned to look.

Sliding off his horse, Will dropped the reins and drew his pistol. Walking with his head on a swivel, he approached the red stain near the fire pit. Gid circled around the opposite side, stepping through the pile of scattered supplies.

"Here's another," he said, kneeling at his discovery. Looking over at Will, he cocked his head. "Where are the bodies?"

"Follow the signs. The ground looks disturbed." He stood and followed his eyes. "They were dragged."

"They?"

"A-yuh. I'm seeing two separate drag paths."

Gid stood and studied the ground near his finding. "It's not the same over here. Looks like whoever it was dragged themselves to this point." He pointed at the large stain on the ground. "From here, I dunno. Maybe they were dragged or helped up. If'n this one got away, ya'd think there'd only be two horses left tied up, an' I'm countin' three."

Heel over toe, Will followed the drag marks away from camp, tracking the blood trail over rockier surfaces. Gid looked to the sky, watching. Buzzards soared close by, their necks twisting, their beady eyes glaring at their new competition. The drag path turned to a smooth plastering of stones marking the way to a sheer drop-off into an adjacent canyon. Will approached the ledge, stopping when he heard a low, ragged gasp carried up from the depths.

"You hear that, Gid?"

"I heard." He moved quickly to join Will at the ledge.

"Hrrrerrgghr."

"It's comin' from over the edge," Gid said.

Peering over the side, a mix of disgust and anger swept over Gid. "Son of a bitch! Look at the bodies, Will."

"Ooooovvrr. Hrrrerrgghr."

Will leaned further, straining to find the source of the sound. "Jesus," he said, pointing. "Right there."

Wedged ten feet below between a boulder and the dead limbs of a mesquite splitting from between the rocks was a man.

"Run and get the rope, Gid. That man is alive."

CHAPTER THIRTY-EIGHT

THE HORIZON MELTED BENEATH A BLOOD-RED SKY, FLAMES of last light fanning over the terrain in shoots of turbulent orange, its radiance dodging darkened shadows that reached up from the depths like vicious claws searching for prey. Were it not for the immediate rescue of the injured man, it would have been a sunset to celebrate. Instead, it was the catalyst fighting against Will and Gid as they hurried to act before they were all swallowed by night and unable to see.

"Make sure that safety line is tight, Will. Ya don't wanna be pullin' us both outta this pit."

"You're good to go, Gid. Even you aren't big enough to drag the horses over the edge."

Will held the reins of both horses and gave a thumbs-up. Tugging at the rope tied around his waist and secured to the horns of both saddles, Gid looked over the edge and puffed a ready breath.

"Hang on there, mister. We're gonna help ya up."

The man groaned a reply. He was fading fast.

Regardless of their rescue attempt, it may already be too late.

Gid glanced back at Will, his silhouette outlined against the crimson dusk. With a ready nod, he eased back until the rope held his weight.

Here we go, Gid thought. *This rope better do its job, er things'll get pretty messy.*

Step by step, Gid descended the rocky cliff, the horses above guiding him down under Will's direction.

"A little more, Will. Almost there," Gid called out as he worked his way lower.

With his boots clinging to the edge like a spider inching its way across its web, Gid positioned himself to land behind the man. From above, there was no way of knowing the extent of his injuries, but one thing was clear, the man would not be able to climb out unassisted.

The rope rubbing the ridge was unsettling, dislodging tiny stones that bounced off Gid before plummeting into the canyon.

"Whoa!" Gid's voice rose from below. "That's good, Will."

The line jerked, pulling Gid away from the man as they dangled side by side. Like a human pendulum, he swung back, reaching for a scraggly branch jutting from the tangle of limbs cradling the injured man. Looking at the spot, Gid shook his head, then glanced below. The rock beneath him was covered with blood.

"Mister, I ain't got a clue how ya ended up here, but it's clear ta me that someone upstairs ain't done with ya yet."

Gid pulled himself closer, gripping the branch like an iron clamp as the rope held taut.

"Listen up." Gid's voice was direct. "I'm gonna slip a rope beneath yer arms and tie ya off ta me. We've got horses above that'll pull us up. All ya have ta do is hold on."

Gid could hear the man breathing, but his concern deepened when he did not answer.

Edging closer, Gid saw that the man's skin was pale as wet clay. From above, he knew the man was in bad shape. But now, face-to-face, Gid knew the truth. There was no time. He had to act fast to save him.

"He ain't lookin' too good, Will. I'll call out when I've got 'im. Just be ready with the horses, ya hear?"

"I hear you, Gid. We'll pull when you say the word."

Gid worked fast. He unwound a secondary rope looped over his shoulder and ran the free end beneath the man's right arm and over his chest. His left side was pinned against the jutting boulder.

"Easy, mister. Gotta slip this rope beneath ya."

Gid moved his grip from the branch to the man's waist, then grabbed his shoulder with his free hand. Gid tugged at the man's body to free some space between him and the rock on which he was wedged.

"Ahhh!" The man responded with a painful yell, his agony falling into the growing shadows of the canyon.

"I hear ya, but there ain't no alternative."

Gid continued, ignoring the man's grunts and groans until the rope appeared. He slid it the rest of the way around and secured it with a bowline, ensuring it would hold firm without tightening around the man's chest. Sliding his arm under the slack end, he lifted the man just enough to test the knot's strength.

Satisfied, Gid looked up to the canyon rim. "Okay, Will. Pull!"

As the rope tightened and fibers stretched under the strain, Gid whispered a quick prayer, then spoke to the man. "Hold on, here we go."

The rope yanked at Gid's waist and bit into the man's underarms, ripping a raw shriek from his lips. His body went limp beside Gid's as they dangled against the cliff, ten feet from safety and over thirty feet above certain death.

Working together, the horses pulled the two men.

"Keep 'em goin'," Gid said as his head popped above the ledge. "This guy needs all the help he can git."

One foot more, then two. Gid clawed his way over the edge, boots scraping against the rock, but the man still dangled below, his weight pulling against the rope.

"Help me drag him up," Gid said.

Will halted the horses, loosed the reins, and dashed to the edge. Leaning over, careful to keep his footing, he grabbed one of the man's arms. Gid grabbed the other, and with a final heave, they hauled him over the edge.

Gid unknotted the ropes, freeing the man from his makeshift harness.

"Let's get him over to the camp," Will said. "I'll stir up the coals and see if I can get some flames going to boil water. Take his arms. I'll grab his feet."

"We better work fast," Gid said, moving to the man's head. "This fella may be off the cliff, but he ain't outta the woods."

Lifting both ends, the brothers carried the man back to camp and laid him close to the fire ring. Gid pulled his knife from his belt and went right to work, cutting away the man's shirt to uncover his injury. Will added scraps of trash, repositioned a few logs atop the coals, then jogged to the horses to retrieve his water pouch and a small pot to place on the fire. By the time he returned, the logs had caught again, crackling and spitting fresh sparks and gray smoke.

Gid resheathed his knife. Will knelt by the fire and poured water into a small metal pot to boil.

"He's lost a lot of blood," Gid said, inspecting the man's injury. "But he may be better off than we first thought."

"How so?" Will asked, setting the pot on the edge of the fire. "Looks like a bullet wound from here."

"Ya ain't wrong about that, Will. He's been shot all right, but I'll be damned if he ain't tougher than an old boot. Look here." Gid pointed to a hole just below the man's ribs. "The bullet went in here." He rolled the man onto his side. "An' here's another hole, just off to the side. See how the edges are blown outward? Damn thing bounced off his ribs and tore out clean. Lucky bastard. It coulda chewed up his insides."

Gid gently laid the man back down.

"Aside from a nasty gash on his left arm, I figure with a little rest, an' if he can avoid infection, he may just pull through."

The fire grew, its flames reaching upward, stealing the last of the sunset's crimson glow and casting it into the ring of stones, where watchful eyes lingered in the flickering light. The soft gurgle of rolling bubbles within the pot and the steam evaporating as it rose signaled the water was ready.

Gid dipped two strips of cloth, cut from the man's shirt, into the boiling water, then dangled them over the pot until they stopped dripping. He gave them a moment to cool, ensuring they would not scald the man's skin, before pressing them against his wounds.

Dry beds of brown crust trailed from the bullet holes, streaking down the man's side. Gid wiped away the blood with one rag while pressing the other firmly over the wounds. Once the area was clean, he lifted the cloths and reexamined the injury. Blood pooled from the openings, spilling into fresh trails that trickled down the man's skin.

"Gotta stop this bleedin'," Gid said. "Here." He pulled his knife from his belt again, flipped it in the air, and caught it by the blade. Holding it out, he said, "Heat the tip. It'll hurt somethin' fierce, but it'll seal the wound."

Will took the knife and slipped the tip into a glowing patch of coals. After a few minutes, he wrapped his hand with a rag from his pocket and removed the knife.

The steel tip burned orange, its edges rimmed in black. Moving around the fire, he knelt beside Gid next to the man.

"He's out now, but may come hollerin' back the second we do this. I'll hold 'im down. You do the rest."

Will nodded. Gid braced the man.

It was not the first time either of them had been forced to cauterize a wound. During the war, it had been a last resort. Gunshot wounds. Severed limbs. The searing heat of an iron tool was sometimes the only way to stop the bleeding. It was painful. Brutal. Necessary.

Will pressed the knife to the man's wound. Flesh sizzled beneath the glowing steel, the harsh stench of burning meat curling into the air. As expected, the man jolted awake, a raw, piercing scream shattering the quiet.

"Hang in there, mister. Almost done," Gid said, his

voice steady despite the man's thrashing. "One more, an' we're through."

The man writhed, wild-eyed with agony, but Gid held firm. Will did not hesitate. He pressed the blade to the second wound.

A scream tore from the man's throat, as sharp and raw as the first before his body went slack beneath Gid.

"Just as well. Needs ta rest anyway," Gid said, releasing his grip.

Will propped the blade on a fire ring stone to cool, then took a seat on a large rock near the fire. "When he comes around, we'll offer him some water, see if he can tell us who he is and what happened here." He glanced toward the darkened landscape. "Now, all we have to do is wait."

Gid stood, rolling his shoulders, but the motion froze as his gaze flicked toward the outer edge of their camp. While they tended to the man, night had swallowed the land. The moon had yet to rise, leaving only the fire's glow to push back the dark.

Then—a sound. The crunch of gravel. The snap of breaking wood.

"Ya hear that, Will?"

Will was already on his feet, hand resting on the grip of his pistol. "I heard."

He stepped up beside Gid. Both men listened, muscles coiled, eyes scanning the blackness beyond the fire's reach.

Another branch cracked.

Gid exhaled, eyes narrowing at the dark.

"We're not alone."

CHAPTER THIRTY-NINE

"I CAIN'T SEE A DAD-GUMMED THING, SULLY. FEELS LIKE we're swimmin' through soup. Why'd we have ta push past sundown?"

Tater followed Sully, shifting in his saddle. His stomach grumbled, his nerves stretched thin.

"Moon'll be up soon enough. That should give us enough light ta see where we're goin'," Sully said. "'Til then, do me a favor, will ya?"

Reluctant to do anything for Sully but too afraid of the consequences to refuse, Tater pulled alongside him. "What ya wantin' me ta do?"

Sully yanked the reins, halting his horse, then leaned over and grabbed Tater by the collar.

"I want ya ta shut the hell up. No more whinin', no more questions. Hear me, Tater? I want ya ta stay that way 'til I say otherwise. Yer the reason we're movin' through the night. Yer the reason those men were kilt. Ya just couldn't keep yer damn yap shut."

A rush of anxiety washed through Tater, swirling with guilt and loathing, thick enough to choke him, but he swallowed it hard. He saw only the pale blur of Sully's eyes. He felt the sharp tug at his neck and smelled the stench of his breath. Clenching his teeth, he stayed still, trapped in his brother's grip. Had there been light, Sully would have sneered at Tater's reaction, but the darkness let him hide his fear.

Sully let go of him, then urged his horse forward as if all was right in the world.

"Come on, chickadee," he said, his voice bouncing with twisted delight.

Tater gulped. He straightened his crumpled clothing and tightened his grip on the reins.

Ain't many straws left 'til ya pull the last one, Sully.

Tater nudged his horse forward, his gut twisting.

If I weren't such a damn coward, maybe I'd—

Sully's voice rose with an off-key, sing-song tune, cutting off Tater and disrupting the night.

"Chickadee, chickadee,

"Holy moses, chickadee,

"They gots my money, wait an' see.

"I'll get it back fer my chickadee."

Sully sang the same four lines again and again as they traveled deeper into the night, the words burrowing into Tater's mind like an itch he could not scratch.

CHAPTER FORTY

ON NIGHTS WHEN THE MOON HAS YET TO RISE, THE barren landscapes of Texas sink into their darkest hours. And within that blackness, when sounds and distant echoes dare to break the silence, a single, brooding question lingers, one as old as night itself: What is out there?

Watching. Listening. Will and Gid stood still, waiting for the answer.

"Stay alert, Gid. It's probably nothing."

"Oh, it's somethin' all right," Gid muttered. "The way the past few days have gone, I can feel that it's definitely somethin'."

Will scanned the perimeter, but all remained quiet.

"I'm gonna slip inta the soup," Gid said, voice low. "See if I can encourage whatever *it* is to either get the hell outta here or show itself."

Will nodded. "Be careful."

Gid crouched, then slipped into the shadows, disappearing from view.

Easing back toward the fire and the sleeping man,

Will returned to the rock he had been using as a stool and sat, his gaze locked on the darkness.

Whatever—or whoever—you are, if I know Gid, you won't remain a mystery for long.

A shifting log in the fire snapped, sending embers spiraling into the night. The dry wood hissed as the flames gnawed at its core.

Will glanced at the man lying unconscious but alive on the ground near the flickering glow. His chest rose and fell in a steady rhythm, a quiet reassurance that told the world no matter what had happened, he was not done here yet.

At once, a loud, high-pitched shriek cut through the night like a banshee fleeing across the plains.

Will jumped to his feet, pistol in hand, muscles coiled, eyes scanning the darkness.

Silence followed.

No snarls. No gunshots. Not a peep more from the pitch-black perimeter.

Where are you, Gid?

Seconds dragged by, slow as the ticking of a faulty grandfather clock. Then—

Clink.

The sound of iron against rock.

Faint at first. Then louder.

With rhythm.

Emerging from the shadows, Gid walked into camp, leading a horse by the reins, concern etched across his face.

"Ya ain't never gonna believe this, Will. Look who I found," Gid said. "Or maybe I should say, who found us."

Appearing in the firelight, sitting atop the horse, was Henry.

Gid led them in as Will stepped forward. They exchanged a questioning glance, then Will turned to the boy. "What in the hell are you doing way out here, Henry? You were supposed to be on a train to Amarillo with your mother and sisters."

Henry slid off the horse, his face smudged with dirt, exhaustion dulling his eyes. "I know. An' I was. But—"

He spoke with urgency, but Will raised a hand. "Slow down. Catch your breath. Gid's gonna tie up your horse while we find a seat near the fire. Once he joins us, you can tell the whole story."

As Gid led the horse away, Will motioned for Henry to sit near the fire and handed him a water pouch. The boy took a long draw.

"Go easy. Don't wanna make yourself sick," Will cautioned.

Gid returned and planted his hands on his hips. "Ain't safe fer ya ta be this far out in the wilderness on yer own, Henry. What's got under yer skin?"

Henry's eyes flicked between Will and Gid, then landed on the man lying on the ground near the fire. "Is he—?"

Will sat across from him, watching the boy's face in the firelight. "Tell us, Henry. Why are you out here?"

Taking a deep breath, Henry explained. "Everythin' was goin' just like it was supposed to. Faith, Grace, me an' Ma made it inta town with time ta spare before the train arrived. Saba ran along, too, but disappeared huntin' a rabbit on the outskirts. Ma bought tickets fer everyone, then went ta see the sheriff. I stayed back to unload the wagon with my sisters until she came back.

When she finally did, she told me I had to sell the wagon an' the horse an' that I should do it as quickly as possible. She was actin' kinda strange, maybe unhappy, but I figured it was on account of everythin' that happened. Anyway, I ended up sellin' the wagon to Mr. Amos, the blacksmith, but he didn't need a horse, so I went to the livery instead. That's where everything changed.

"I was standin' at the edge of the livery when I heard voices. One sounded low and mean. Made my stomach turn. I ducked behind a haystack, held my breath. That's when Sheriff Wolfe stormed in with Edgar Hunt behind 'im. The sheriff was angry about somethin'. Then, I heard it. He was mad about somethin' Ma said. Right mad."

Gid took a seat across from Henry. "Edgar Hunt. Who's he?"

"Mr. Hunt owns the livery. He ain't a bad man, but he ain't a good one either. He's always tryin' ta be on everyone's side as long as he gets somethin' out of it."

"We've known men like that," Will said. "Keep going, Henry."

Henry nodded. "So, I was hiding behind a tall haystack when I heard Mr. Hunt ask the sheriff if anyone knew that he was the one who sent those men to our cabin."

"Wait," Gid said. "Let me stop ya right there. Sheriff Wolfe sent those men?"

Henry nodded, jaw clenched. "That's what I heard. Said he was comin' for ya both." Henry paused, swallowing hard. "An' if he couldn't find ya? He'd take Ma instead. Haul her back from Amarillo an' blame her for killin' them. I couldn't let that happen."

Henry's hands curled into fists. "I stayed as quiet as a mouse, tryin' ta hear anythin' else, but alls I heard was the sheriff tellin' Mr. Henry ta get the horses ready. An', that once they settled with the undertaker, he an' his deputies would be after ya. I slipped out soon as I could. The train whistle was blowin', but I weren't gettin' on it. Not without warnin' y'all first."

Will and Gid shared a glance, but neither said a word.

"Mr. Amos, the blacksmith, had my horse tied up in front of his shop, so I ran again, but not for the depot. I loosed the rope, threw myself on the horse, and kicked. No saddle. No time to care. Just ridin' hard, grippin' tight, tryin' not to fall. My legs burned, my hands ached, but I didn't stop. Couldn't. When I made it back ta the cabin, I rushed to throw together a few supplies, found an old saddle in the shed, and stole some jerky outta one of the dead man's saddlebag. Saba must have seen me ridin' fer home 'cause there she was waitin' on the porch like always when I finally saddled up ta leave.

"I set out fer the spot where Pa was shot but I weren't alone. Heard hooves. Dropped low in the saddle, slipped into the brush. Just in time, too. Sheriff Wolfe, his men, the undertaker, Hunt, all of 'em were ridin' out toward our cabin.

"When they were out of sight, I looked for tracks that led away, like someone was runnin'. Ya know. Not normal prints headin' fer town or stayin' on the regular trail."

Henry took a breath and let a smile crinkle the edge of his lips. "Pa taught us to track deer and squirrel, me an' my brother, I mean, before he died. That all stopped after." Henry paused, drifting out of thought, possibly into a fond memory, but it did not last. He wiped his nose, straightened his posture, and continued his story.

"I figured if I could follow deer tracks, I could follow horse prints, so that's what I did. Saba ran alongside until we came to a stream. I stopped ta water the horse, still sittin' in the saddle, when I heard it. A low growl. My gut went cold. I looked up, an' there it was—yellow eyes glarin' at me through the trees. It showed its teeth an' hissed. The horse stomped its feet, real nervous-like. Snortin', too. I grabbed my pistol an' fired. Missed. Fired again. Still missed.

"Saba's always been a good dog. She lunged, teeth bared, snarlin'. Made me remember why Pa called her Killer. The mountain lion hesitated, then took off. Saba chased it into the brush. Left me there, breathin' hard, hands shakin', wonderin' if I'd just used up all my luck. Tuckin' the pistol in my belt, I grabbed the reins and took off, me an' the horse runnin' fast as we could, crossin' when the water grew shallow. It was all I could think ta do. I didn't have a place to go or hide. I followed the water on the opposite side and happened upon prints that I thought looked similar ta the ones I'd been trackin', but there was no tellin' fer sure. With Saba nowhere in sight and the sun gettin' lower, I set out again, followin' the new tracks.

"Weren't long before I found a deserted camp an' what looked like a grave. I didn't stick around though. Probably should'a. I still ain't seen any signs of Saba. She's a pretty smart dog, an' I don't think that lion got the best of her. My guess is she headed back ta the cabin, but I ain't goin' back there for a while. Anyhow, it was already late, I didn't know how far behind the sheriff and his posse were, an' I wasn't gonna give up lookin' fer y'all. If the shoe were on the other foot, I figured you'd do the same.

"When the sun set, I walked the horse. It was real slow goin', but I guess I got lucky again. I saw the glow of a fire an' headed straight for it."

Will shifted in his seat. "I agree, Henry," he said. "You were very lucky. Not every campfire you come across is always a welcome one."

"Yer right," Henry said. "But I found ya." He turned to Gid. "Or like ya said...you found me." Henry stood, eyes wide, reflecting the dancing flames before him. "Either way, sheriff's comin'. An' from the sounds of it, he ain't stoppin' 'til he finds ya or goes after Ma. What are we gonna do?"

CHAPTER FORTY-ONE

AN EFFERVESCENT GLOW ROLLED OVER THE TERRAIN, painting everything in its path a soft white and pale blue, a primordial reflection of the late, languid moon. Will and Gid spoke softly while watching shadows appear on the horizon and over the earth where jagged canyons lay still like a trap waiting for prey.

"The kid's damn crazy fer ridin' out here alone," Gid said, glancing over his shoulder. Henry lay by the fire, opposite the unconscious man, and slept.

"A-yuh, but he's only doing what he felt was right, crazy or not," Will said. "What's more important is what he said about the sheriff and how he's placing the blame on us. Henry and Liza are the only witnesses. If Wolfe has a personal stake in this beyond just the money owed, and I assume he does, this could get out of hand real quick if we aren't careful."

Gid leaned forward and spat. "What's the plan, then?" he asked.

"Well, the way I see it, we've gotta prioritize a few things. If our injured friend pulls through, I feel obligated to get him home. Can't leave him to go it alone. Then, there's the killers. We're close, but..."

Gid chimed in, "The longer we delay, the farther they can run an' most likely disappear."

"Right." Will turned, taking in the dwindling fire, Henry, the string of horses secured together, and the injured man. "We started this hunt able to go as fast and as careful as we liked. With all this in tow"—Will gestured to the camp—"things just got more complicated."

Gid nodded. "And with Wolfe on our tail, all bets are off."

Will faced Gid. "If we can make it to sunup without any more surprises or complications, we may have a fighting chance to stay in front of all this and still get back on the killers' trail."

"That's just it though, right, Will?" Gid paused, fire-light flickering across his face. "Complications? Hell, that's what we do best."

CHAPTER FORTY-TWO

FRESH WARMTH SHOT ACROSS THE TERRAIN AS THE SUN crested the horizon, its bright yellow and orange burn battling billowing white clouds gathering in the east. The large, cotton-like clusters deflected the early rays, their edges glowing before catapulting beams across the state. Will and Gid had been up since dawn, but the morning brought more than just the rising sun, it brought a voice.

"You fellas the ones that pulled me off the cliff?"

Will and Gid were preparing the horses when their injured friend spoke for the first time.

"Mornin' stranger," Gid said. "Weren't too sure ya'd pull through. Curious though 'bout what happened."

"Two sons of bitches, that's what happened." The man tried to sit up, a painful grimace twisted his face.

Gid rushed over to help him. Reaching out, the man gripped Gid's arm as he fought to steady himself. It took a moment, but he finally found his balance, his breath coming in shallow bursts. Gid guided him back until he could lean against a saddle propped near the fire, his body sagging with exhaustion. He let out a slow exhale, wincing as fresh pain rolled through him.

"The name's Stanton. Bill Stanton. I work for Hank Wilson over at the Triple Bar S. You fellas came along just in time."

"I'm Will. This is my brother Gid," he said, gesturing to Gid. "I'd say we were late." Will knelt by the fire and poked at the coals, repositioning a pot of water set to boil. "Care to tell us how you ended up on the side of the cliff?"

Stanton shifted, straightening his torso and biting his bottom lip to quell the pain.

"It was the middle of the day yesterday and these two fellas come ridin' in from the south. They seemed friendly enough. One had a way about him that didn't set right, but we all overlooked it. The other? Hell, looking back, he must have been the least threatening man in the West. Trouble was, the one we should have been paying closer attention to got the drop on us when Ben Reed, one of our men, questioned him about the hat he was wearing. Turns out those boys had a hat and saddle from our boss and were trying to sell it to us. Based on what happened next, I'm afraid that they might have done the same to Mr. Wilson."

Nearby, Henry stirred, drawn out of sleep by the conversation. Blinking against the morning light, he sat up, his gaze shifting to the injured man across from him.

"Gid?" Henry said, looking at who had been the unconscious man. "He's alive?"

Stanton smiled and chuckled. He coughed painfully, eyes landing on Henry. "Sure as shootin', young man. You ride in with these men?"

Henry's eyes flicked to Will and then back to Gid. "Well, not exactly."

"Mr. Stanton," Will said. "I hate to agree with you, but Gid and I came across a camp southeast of here. We found a man who had been shot and killed. Rounded up what we assumed was his horse, then buried him before heading this way." Will stood and threw a branch on the fire. "Those men who killed your friends and left you for dead killed this boy's father over near Clarendon and have been on the run. Me and Gid have been tracking them since yesterday."

"Trackin' blind, too," Gid added. "Don't have a face or a name ta go on. Just the tracks the bastards left behind."

"I know their voices," Henry said, sitting up. "That's all though. Pa had me hide in the wagon before we got close enough ta talk to 'em. Then, ya know. *It* happened. The blast scared the horse and it bolted away with me in the back of the wagon before I could get a look."

Stanton gazed at the boy, nodding as if understanding the loss Henry had endured.

"Son, I am sorry about your pa," Stanton said, then shifted his attention back to Will, "But I think I know a thing or two that'll help you find those fellers."

Gid and Will shared a glance.

"One's name is Tater. Mousy fella. He wasn't the one who started all the shooting and killing. The other's the one that's calling the shots. His name is Sully, but he might well have been the devil in old boots. He got the drop on all of us, shooting Ben Reed and then Earl Clack, our trail boss. Tater looked scared as the day is long, but the son of a bitch shot me before I could get a bead on Sully. I don't remember much else but the crazy laughter and singing I heard and then being dragged along the ground toward the ledge over yonder. It was a horrible thing. Ben and Earl were good men."

"Knowin' their names'll help, but it'll take time trackin' them boys through these parts," Gid said. "What with all the rocky terrain an' all. They coulda gone anywhere from here."

Stanton smiled. "Well, let me tell you something that'll make the hunt a hell of a lot easier—*Tascosa, Texas*. That's where they're headed. Before things turned south, they said they were looking for work but had business to see to in Tascosa first."

"Mr. Stanton, that's news worth hearing this morning, but first things first. You said you work for the Triple Bar S?" Will said.

"That's right," Stanton said. "Near thirty years now."

Will crossed his arms. "Me and Gid will get you back to the ranch, then resume the manhunt."

"Gentlemen, I appreciate it, but I couldn't—"

Gid moved next to Will, nodding. "A man ridin' alone with four horses an' a gunshot wound over this terrain? Cain't be leavin' ya to fend for yerself in that shape. Wouldn't be right."

"Mr. Stanton," Will said. "Now that we know who they are and where they're headed, we've got the edge. That gives us time to get you home safe. I just hate that the price for the information was so damn high."

"What about Sheriff Wolfe?" Henry asked, looking between Will and Gid.

"The sheriff?" Stanton looked at Henry, eyes curious to learn more.

"He an' his men are somewhere's behind us. Prob'ly catch up before long."

Stanton pursed his lips as if making a decision. "Boy's right," Stanton said. "You should wait for the sheriff instead of heading on with me."

Gid looked out to the open range, scanning the horizon past the canyons and rolling, rocky knolls, and spoke. "No, it's not like that." Turning, he faced Stanton. "Sheriff Wolfe, he ain't what ya'd call a proper authority. He's lookin' fer us, but fer reasons of his own that ain't got nothin' ta do with the law."

Stanton eyed Will and Gid, his jaw tightening before he cocked his head to relax. "I reckon if you were on the wrong side, I'd still be dangling off that cliff, waiting to die."

Stanton took a deep breath and started to stand, wobbling on weakened legs. Gid leaped over the fire ring and caught him before he lost his balance.

"Why don't ya take a load off, Mr. Stanton." Gid said, bracing him under his arm. "Regain some strength before movin' so much."

"Nope, though I must admit, an escort might be exactly what I need right now." Stanton coughed and grimaced, then gritted his teeth and found his footing. "Daylight's burning, Gid, and you boys have a job to do."

Stanton's gaze flicked east. The white tufts of clouds had darkened, flashes of lightning sparking within, though still too distant to hear the rumble. He exhaled, steadying himself. "If those clouds are any sign of what's coming, we best get to riding. Storm's rolling in."

Gid looked at Will. "And that ain't the only one."

CHAPTER FORTY-THREE

SULLY RODE TALL IN THE SADDLE, LIKE THE GRAND marshal of a Fourth of July parade. Tater brought up the rear, banished to ride drag—his punishment for running his mouth too much and his gun too little. Never mind that he had shot the tall man and saved Sully's life. That did not matter. What mattered to Sully was Tater learning to keep his mouth shut and do as he was told.

Passing beyond the boundaries of the canyons, the trail stretched, dry and winding, cutting through the mesquite and scrub like a scar on the land. The mid-morning sun blazed, baking the earth beneath them. Dust coiled in lazy swirls with each plodding step of their horses. Sully's jaw was set firm, his expression unreadable, while Tater slumped in the saddle, burdened by undeserved blame.

Sully threw a quick glance over his shoulder, just enough to ensure Tater was not falling behind. Tater's face was set in a stubborn glare, his lips pressed tight, but he kept pace. Sully gave a small, satisfied nod, his craving for control settling over both the living and the dead.

The silence stretched between them, broken only by the rhythmic creak of leather and the occasional grunt of their horses. Ahead, the horizon shimmered with heat, but within that wavy glaze, buildings came into view. Sully curled his lips, twisted elation and brazen certainty in his gut. Redemption was close enough to taste, stoking his hunger to settle scores and stuff his pockets once they reached town.

Sully, testing Tater's attention and resolve, raised his voice like a barker outside Buffalo Bill Cody's Wild West show. "Listen up, boys an' girls. That means you, Tater. We got ourselves civilization ahead. Remember yer place, an' follow the plan, an' we'll come out richer than John Chisum or Richard King on the other side."

Tater stared at the back of Sully's head, mumbling to himself. "They may be rich, but they're both dead."

Not hearing Tater's remarks, Sully sang his own praises, his mind lost to his new outlook on life, craving the rush of taking lives and the insatiable pull of vengeance.

CHAPTER FORTY-FOUR

THERE WAS LITTLE GIVE IN THE SADDLE. THE RHYTHMIC clop and sway of Bill Stanton's horse's rolling gait sent sharp pains through his torso, but he never once complained.

The trail to the Triple Bar S wound around the rims of three separate canyons, each like the ragged claw of an enormous hand sunken into the earth. With Stanton leading the way and Will close behind, they rode single file until they circumvented the last of the jagged holes and reached open ground.

Will pulled alongside Stanton's left while Henry and Gid flanked him on the right, leading the packed horses of the deceased men. Curious how Henry had gotten tangled up in the manhunt, Stanton talked mostly with the boy as they ambled along. Will and Gid listened as Henry recalled events, beginning with the killing of his father, the attack by the men at the cabin, and his discovery of Sheriff Wolfe's dark and dangerous side. Stanton had taken Will and Gid at their word, but hearing Henry corroborate what he had already heard from the Crocketts only reinforced his trust in them. By the time Henry had finished, Stanton had already made up his mind about his companions.

He pulled back the reins, stopping his horse. The others pulled up alongside him. Twisting and grimacing until his body adjusted to its new position, Stanton looked at Henry, then reached out his hand. "You're one brave young man, Henry Morgan."

A bit confused but appreciating the compliment, Henry took Stanton's hand and shook. "Thank you, sir."

"Look over yonder, Henry," Stanton said, releasing his grip to point at the horizon. "If you look carefully enough, you can see some black specks scattered about. That'd be Triple Bar S cattle. We're only a couple of miles out. Once we get to the ranch and pass along the bad news, I'll have our cook rustle you up a proper breakfast. How's that sound?"

At the mention of food, Henry's stomach growled before he could answer. Gid leaned over and slapped him on the back.

"Watch out fer this one, Bill. I've seen him eat 'bout a hundred pies in one sittin'."

Henry spun toward Gid, edging an embarrassed smile. "It weren't a hundred. That was you."

The men chuckled. Stanton braced his arm across his ribs and winced but nodded a warm glance at Henry. "Don't know that we'll have that many, but I have seen our cook stack pancakes so high that the pile near about fell over. Think you could handle something like that?"

"And how," Henry said, licking his lips.

Will glanced over his shoulder, scanning the terrain. The sky continued to blacken, clouds churning taller in the day's heat, swallowing more of the clear, bright blue with every passing moment. "If we're as close as you say, Bill, let's keep up the pace, as long as you can stand it."

"I'll be fine. Just give me a second to get situated."

Will shot Gid a glance, lifting his chin and flicking his eyes toward the trail behind them—an unspoken communication to be on the lookout. Gid answered with a knowing nod.

After a moment, Stanton signaled he was ready, and they nudged their horses onward, continuing across the open range. Lingering a horse length behind, Gid kept a watchful eye on the path behind them, the threatening clouds above and a faint, distant smudge that hovered between earth and sky, shifting like a pack of dust devils dancing across the prairie.

By late morning, and after passing through several small groups of ranging cattle, a cluster of small ranch-style buildings dotted the horizon behind a long line of fence posts spread out across the wide terrain. Drawing nearer, Henry noticed the fencing and was the first to speak up. "What's with all the wire, Mr. Stanton? I see the posts, but it looks like a spider's web is holdin' 'em together."

His curiosity revealed more than just his sheltered upbringing. It also showed his keen sense of observation, which impressed Stanton.

"Henry, you're looking at wire fencing. Out here, wood is harder to come by, so fencing off an area as large as the one you see wouldn't be possible if it weren't for the wire."

"Barbed wire, Henry," Will added. "About ten years ago, a couple different men came up with the idea, but it wasn't until a man named Joseph Glidden perfected it that it really caught on. Now, ranchers can fence off land to keep their cattle from free-grazing, though sometimes they'll do both."

"Like the Triple Bar S," Stanton added. "Just depends on the size of our herd, the time of year, and the weather."

"Won't they just push through?" Henry asked.

"Some try, but the barbs are sharp. Cattle feel pain like anything else, you know," Stanton said, pointing to his ribs. "Would you keep rubbing your body up against something like that time and again?"

Henry shook his head. "No, I guess I wouldn't."

Squinting, Henry tried to get a better look, but they were still too far away to make out the sharp, nasty bite of the fencing's barbs. As he gazed ahead, he saw something else to question. "Who are they?" He pointed at two riders approaching.

Stanton leaned forward, eyes narrowing, then relaxed and raised a hand over his head. Looking at the riders, he spoke with relief in his voice. "Fellas, you did a good job getting me home, but it's best I explain everything once we meet up with them. The men we lost were friends to all of us at the ranch. The news'll hit hard."

"This is your place, Bill. We'll follow your lead," Will said.

Stanton continued to wave at the riders, though his arm grew heavy and pain throbbed through his ribs. When the riders came close enough for their faces to be seen, their expressions darkened at the sight of the empty horses and the strangers accompanying their friend.

They pulled to a halt in front of Stanton's horse,

eyeing Will and Gid with caution. They both wore similar clothing, though their hats were different designs. One wore a cattleman style hat with a bold leather hatband affixed with an oval turquoise stone. The other wore an odd-style slouch hat with a feather tucked into a beaded hat band.

"Bill," the man with the stone said.

"Randall," Stanton replied, then looked at the man with the feather. "Jack."

Jack nodded, then spoke, his voice carrying an unfamiliar yet melodious drawl. "Saw ya comin', mate. Where's the rest?"

Stanton took a deep breath, bracing his side again with his arm, before responding. "Had the wool pulled over our eyes by a couple men yesterday."

Both Randall's and Jack's palms slid toward their gun belts, their eyes shifting to Will and Gid.

"Not them," Stanton urged. "These fellas saved my life. Let's head to the house. I need to tell Martha the bad news."

"Earl?" Randall said.

Stanton nodded.

"Ben?"

Stanton nodded again.

Jack relaxed his arm, resting it on the saddle horn. "Well, Mr. Wilson wasn't with ya. We should ride out ta meet 'im. Make sure he's—"

"Pretty sure he's gone, too, Jack."

"How can ya know that?"

Stanton gestured to the brothers. "Boys, this is Will and Gid Crockett. The boy's name is Henry Morgan." Turning to Will, he continued, "Will, how about you tell them what you told me."

It took only a few minutes for Will to retell the story, each detail jarring to the men hearing it for the first time, and just as painful for Stanton.

Randall and Jack listened intently, their demeanor shifting to anger as the story unfolded. When Will finished, and after taking a moment to let everything sink in, Jack spoke up, his frustration directed at Will. "From the sounds of it, yer gonna keep goin' until ya track 'em down. The killers, yeah?" Will started to speak, but Jack was not finished. "Mr. Wilson was the only man that took a chance on me when I arrived in this country. I knew horses and cattle, but bein' a bushman and a drover down under didn't matter. Only thing that did was my bein' from the other side of the world. I was a Sydney duck. A kangaroo cowboy. A foreigner. Mr. Wilson gave me a place ta stay and food ta eat. If one of us had been with 'im"—Jack gestured to Randall—"he'd still be alive today. When it comes right down to it, once you're off again, I'm comin' along."

Jack stared at Will, breathing deeply in and out of his nose.

"Hold on there, Jack," Stanton said, eyes narrowed. "We ain't barely home, and there's more going on of which you are not yet aware." He turned to Will. "Sorry about that. I told you the news'll hit hard. We're a close bunch here at the Triple Bar S."

"No, sir. No apologies necessary," Will replied, eyes glued to Jack. "Your friend here has conviction. If I were in his shoes, I'd feel the same way." Glancing at Gid, he continued. "As for joining the hunt, maybe we have a drink first and talk about it."

Eyeing one another, Will watched Jack's clenched jaw relax, followed by a single nod. "I can live with that,"

Jack said, then turned to Randall. "Lead the way home an' let's get Bill off his horse and somewhere he can rest. Sound good?"

"I won't argue with that," Stanton replied.

With Randall and Jack leading the way, the group rode toward the ranch. Though the sting of bad news lingered, the steady rhythm of hooves and the sight of buildings in the distance eased some of the tension.

Stanton shifted in his saddle with a grimace, one arm pressed tight against his ribs. "I'll tell you what," he grunted, "I ain't been this sore since that bull tossed me clean over the rail back in '77."

Jack chuckled, glancing over his shoulder. "An' you still refused to admit you were drunk when it happened."

"Because I wasn't," Stanton fired back, though the crooked grin on his face said otherwise.

Even Randall cracked a smile. "You were too drunk to stand straight. We near had to roll you onto that wagon just to git ya back to the bunkhouse, Bill."

"Well, hell. That was a long time ago. Ain't how I remember it."

The laughter that followed was not loud or long, but it broke the edge that had been hanging over them since the news of Hank, Ben, and Earl. Even Henry, leading one of the empty horses, found himself smiling despite everything.

Will let the banter flow, feeling the weight in the air lighten. He glanced over at Gid, who rode steady with the other empty horses in tow. Gid caught his eye and gave a faint nod—this was what they needed.

"NOT MUCH FARTHER," Randall called out, tipping his hat toward a cluster of outbuildings ahead. A main house came into view, along with a barn offset by two corrals, a bunkhouse, and a series of smaller open-air structures opposite the main corral. Smoke curled from a chimney atop the house, its thin trail cutting into the midday sky.

When they reached the ranch, Randall whistled, then waved, hailing a couple of hands who were working a horse in the corral. Pulling up to a hitching post in front of the house, Randall and Jack swung down from the saddle, secured their horses, then attended to Stanton. Across the yard, the hands hurried over, their boots kicking up dust behind them.

"What's wrong with Bill?" one asked. "He take a hit?"

"Nothing I can't shake off," Stanton answered, though the way he labored getting out of the saddle said otherwise.

"Let's get you inside," Randall said. "And someone bring whiskey—strong stuff."

Bill swung down with a grunt, leaning on Jack for a beat before waving him off. "I still got two good legs."

"Barely," Jack muttered with a grin.

"And it's too early for whiskey. I promised the boy some good eatin' once we arrived."

"You sure you didn't take a blow to the head, there, Bill? It's always a good time for whiskey." Randall smirked, his jest cutting through the tension of mounting curiosity from the other hands.

Will and Gid dismounted, their boots hitting the dirt with a solid thud. As Gid untied the straps holding the two horses he had been leading, one of the ranch hands approached and took the reins, leading the horses away. Will turned just in time to catch Henry glancing around, clearly unsure of what to do next.

"Henry," Will called, pointing to the ranch hand with the horses. "You did good today. Hop down and follow along with Mr. Wilson's horse. He'll show you where she goes."

Henry slid off his horse, secured the reins to the hitching post like he had seen the others do, then untied the knotted rope around the saddle horn.

"Come on," Will added. "Let's not fall behind."

Henry nodded and led the horse after the ranch hand.

Will started after the others toward the house but hesitated when he noticed Gid walking away, his eyes fixed on the distance. He crossed over to him, about to speak, when Gid shifted his gaze and spoke first.

"Ya see that?" He pointed to a hazy smudge stretching along the dark horizon. "Ain't a doubt in my mind what's tossin' that dust, Will. Henry was right about Sheriff Wolfe. He ain't too far behind."

CHAPTER FORTY-FIVE

INSIDE THE RANCH HOUSE, A SADDENED WHIMPER DRIFTED through the halls, past loyal cowboys with bowed heads and hats in hand. Stanton's voice followed, his soft cadence carrying words of prayer, striving to comfort all who listened. Removing their hats, Will and Gid stepped through the front door, following the sounds into a great room.

Stanton sat on a sofa beside an older woman, his hands cradling her twitching fingers, with Randall, Jack, and the other ranch hands gathered around them. A younger woman stood near a window that overlooked the south side of the Triple Bar S, with a small girl latched onto her leg. Reverence filled the room.

"And now, O Lord, in this time of sorrow, we ask for Your mercy and Your peace. May the words of my mouth and the meditations of our hearts be acceptable in Your sight, O Lord, our strength and our redeemer. Grant comfort to the brokenhearted, peace to the weary, and hope to those left behind. In Your holy name we pray. Amen."

Whispers of Amen trickled from the lips of everyone in the room, the young girl's high-pitched voice rising above the rest.

Gid leaned close to Will. "Where's Henry?"

Will's eyes swept the room, meeting the somber gazes of the others, but Henry was nowhere to be seen. "Guess he hasn't come in yet," Will said.

"Will. Gid," Stanton called out, his voice softer than what it had been on the range. He gestured with an outstretched arm, inviting them over to the sofa. "May I introduce Martha Wilson. Martha, this is Will and Gid Crockett."

"Ma'am," Gid said, managing a polite smile.

"Mrs. Wilson, it's a pleasure to meet you, though I wish it were under different circumstances," Will said.

Still holding Martha's hands, Stanton explained how Will and Gid had saved his life and that they were already on the hunt for the murderers. As he spoke, Martha's gaze hardened, a flicker of fire catching in her eyes. When Stanton finished, she pulled her hands away and stood.

"Are you sure it was my husband that you buried? The land is so vast, it could have been anyone."

Absorbing her hopeful gaze, Will shook his head slowly, regret etched across his face. "Mrs. Wilson, you're right. West Texas is wide open, and it could have been anybody, but it wasn't."

He bowed his head. A heavy silence lingered before he spoke again. "Mr. Stanton confirmed it when he saw Hank's horse in our care." Will paused, the tension of the room thick with watching eyes and listening ears. He started to continue but stopped short. Martha noticed.

"You're holding something back, Mr. Crockett. Out with it."

"Ma'am, it's just that I recognize your face from a picture I found in Hank's pocket." Will lifted his head, eyes connecting with the woman once again. "If there was any other way it was someone else, I would tell you. I am sorry for your loss, Mrs. Wilson."

Biting her bottom lip, she raised a finger to wipe a tear settling in the corner of her eye, then straightened her posture, iron grit rising through her sorrow.

"These men..." She paused, fiddling with her fingers, looking away. "Not that they are truly men, but brigands, fiends..." Turning back to Will and Gid, a fiery look sparked in her eyes. "Do you know where they are headed?"

Gid spoke up, nodding. "Sure do, ma'am."

"Very well. Then some of my men will go with you. If they're as bad as Bill described, you'll need the help."

Will and Gid shared a glance.

"Mrs. Wilson, we..." Will stopped short of finishing when the look in Martha's eyes told him that no matter his excuse, she would have her own dogs in the fight. She arched an eyebrow, waiting. "What I mean to say is that Jack has already volunteered."

Stepping forward, Jack ran a hand over his head to fix his hair, then addressed Mrs. Wilson directly. "I told them I was going along. Didn't give them much choice, really. That is, if you can stand to have me away for a few days, Mrs. Wilson."

Martha cocked her head. "Certainly, Jack." Looking around the room, she added, "And anyone else who wishes to go will have my blessing. We've all lost because of those evil men."

Before Will or Gid could object, Henry burst through the front door shouting.

"Will! Gid! They're here. They're—"

"Whoa there, Henry. Catch yer breath," Gid said.

Concern flashed across Martha's face. Her eyes darted from Gid to Henry, then to Stanton.

"Who's here? Who's this young man that would come yelling into my house?"

"Martha, this is Henry," Stanton said. "He's the reason Will and Gid are out here in the first place. Those men killed his pa."

A swift flush of red filled Martha's cheeks. Her shoulders sagged under the burden of their shared loss.

"Oh, young Henry. It seems we have too much in common. Now, settle down and tell me, who is here?"

"Sheriff Wolfe...ma'am...from town...Clarendon, I mean."

Martha's shoulders relaxed, hope flickering in her eyes. "This is good news. With the sheriff here, he can—"

"It's not as it seems, Mrs. Wilson," Will cut in, his voice firm.

As quickly as hope blossomed within Martha, it was thrust away.

He turned to face Jack, Randall, and the other men who stayed behind after the prayer. "He's got a badge, sure. But he's after us."

Gid stepped forward. "But he's as dirty as the underside of my boot in a cow pasture. Me an' Will protected Henry's ma and sisters when Wolfe's men came callin' not long after we found Henry's pa dead. They're as bad as the killers we're huntin'. And the sheriff? He might be worse."

Looking around the room, Martha narrowed her eyes and barked orders to her men.

"This is my ranch. Will and Gid Crockett are our guests and we are in their debt. Whoever it is riding in, we'll meet them and then send them on their way." Agreeable murmurs swept throughout the room. "If they choose otherwise, we'll deal with them ourselves."

CHAPTER FORTY-SIX

THE PERPETUAL GURGLE AND SHALLOW FLOW OF THE Canadian River fell soft on Tater's ears, its cool waters just as refreshing as he bent down to splash his face. He knelt at the river's edge, closed his eyes as water dripped from his nose, and listened. It calmed him like the hum of a nurturing mother, its melodious whisper, though only a moment in time, was the only stable element in Tater's unruly life.

If there ever was a place like this where I could disappear, I'd take it in a heartbeat, he thought.

Opening his eyes, he rubbed his face, then dipped his hand into the water again. This time, when the cool ran over his cheeks and lips, droplets slipping into his mouth, his euphoric dream was shattered by a mischievous and all-too-familiar cackle. Swiveling his head left and glancing upstream, Tater saw Sully standing ankle-deep in the water with his trousers pulled down and hips extended. A yellow stream arched away from him, splashing with frothy bubbles.

It took only a second to realize that Tater was in a

direct line of fire, the quenching water soiled by Sully's foul spray.

He sprang to his feet, spitting to clear his mouth.

"Goddamnit, Sully! What the hell is wrong with ya!"

Sully pulled up his britches, laughing so hard he almost lost his footing. He stomped out of the water, holding his gut as if he had just been shot.

"You should see the look on yer face, Tater. How's the water tastin'? Refreshing as ever, I bet."

His rising laughter infuriated Tater. As Sully returned to his horse, Tater charged, ramming him from behind. The two slammed into the side of Sully's horse before rebounding backward. The horse let out a sharp squeal, hooves skittering over soggy gravel as throaty growls and scraping boots tumbled in a tangled heap on the riverbank. Tater took the brunt of the fall, the impact knocking the wind out of him as Sully landed hard on top.

"That's it, Tater. I knew'd ya had fight in ya." Scrambling, Sully flipped over, straddling Tater and using both hands to pin him down. "But I ain't the one ya should be tusslin' with little brother."

Using his weight as leverage, Sully squeezed his legs and thrust Tater toward the water's edge. They struggled, but what had been a blindsided attack backfired.

Two more thrusts and drags pulled Tater closer, the gurgling flow lapping the top of his head. He flexed his muscles, but Sully had the upper hand and would not budge.

One more thrust forward and water flowed into Tater's ear.

"How's that feel now, dummy?"

With a brutal heave, Sully shoved Tater deeper into

the current until water rushed over his face. Tater kicked wildly, but Sully would not let up.

"Fight back, Tater. Or cain't ya hear me?"

Sully pulled Tater's head out of the river.

"Fight, I said."

Tater's eyes widened. His heart raced. A mix of water and air spewed from his mouth as he coughed violently beneath Sully's hold.

"No? Back ya go," he said, submerging Tater's head once more.

The gurgle underwater was just as pronounced as above, and for a fleeting moment, Tater considered letting go, succumbing to his brother's wrath and the river's suffocating grip. His fingers loosened. His eyelids fluttered shut. There, in the cold pull of the current, the sensation of freedom, of escape, was within reach. It was not ideal, but anything, even death, seemed better than living in what he felt was hell on earth. His limbs tingled. His mind drifted as calm thoughts formed a fragile barrier between his fading consciousness and the crazed beast above, and for once in as long as he could remember, he began to feel at peace.

With a sudden jolt, as if plucked breech from his mother's womb, Tater was ripped out of the water and tossed onto dry land. Back into hell. His body thudded on the ground, forcing air and water to rush from his lungs. He coughed. Spat. Vomited river water, along with any hope of clinging to that crystalline serenity. Instead, his lungs burned like wildfire. His head pounded. As he opened his eyes, he felt the sting of unrealized tears and silty river grit, trapped in the looming shadow of the devil.

Sully stood over Tater, grinding his teeth as he bent

low, glaring down at him. "I ain't done with ya yet, Tater."

Sully straightened and looked over his shoulder across the river. "That there is Tascosa."

He turned to face his Zion, eyes slitted against the sunlight, sharp as a hawk hunting prey.

"Get up. It's time fer a reckoning."

CHAPTER FORTY-SEVEN

FUNNY THING HOW A STORM CAN SEEM SO FAR OFF, ITS ghostly flashes and thunderous rumble but a distant concern, until, all of a sudden, its towering mass of jagged charcoal clouds, with whipping winds, barrels through, wreaking havoc on everything in its path. Men with evil agendas are not so different. Will and Gid were no strangers to the kind, but even in all their years of experience, they knew the dangers they faced once they stepped outside to face the music.

"Will Crockett. Gid Crockett. Show yourselves and stand for the murders of four men or bear the weight of being named cowards and killers!"

Peering through the front window, Stanton relayed what he saw. "I count four armed men on horseback. Three look seasoned. The other's like a coon caught in the feed bin."

"Crockett!"

Stanton looked back at Will, Gid, and the rest. "I presume that's Sheriff Wolfe. Don't seem to like y'all much. Maybe I should show him the door."

Moving away from the window, Martha blocked his path. "You're in no condition to go outside, Bill. As I said before, this is my ranch. I won't have anyone making threats here. Not on my land. Hank wouldn't have stood for it, and I sure as hell won't either."

Whirling around, Martha marched through a sea of parting ranch hands, each eager to step into the fight. As she passed, they fell in line, Jack and Randall right behind her when she threw open the front door.

Will and Gid started to follow but were called back by Stanton. "This may have started as your problem, but ridin' out here with demands and a show of force just made it ours as well."

"We fight our own battles, Bill," Gid said. "I ain't never been one ta hide from trouble."

"Nobody's hiding, Gid. Soon as Martha has her say, especially with all our men surrounding her, Sheriff Wolfe won't have a leg to stand on."

Gid looked at Will. Over the years, they had faced worse odds under circumstances that seemed impossible to survive. Though numbers were on their side, they knew that staying put was not worth the overall risk.

Will glanced at the ranch hands, fingers twitching near holstered irons, their loyalty undeniable. It was not their fight, but it would be their blood if things went sideways.

"This isn't our ranch," Will muttered to Gid, "but it's our fight. No sense dragging them down with us."

Turning to Stanton, "Bill, keep Henry close. Should the worst happen, make sure he gets to Amarillo and finds his family."

Without waiting for a reply, Will and Gid slipped

through the house, boots heavy on the wooden floor. They pushed through the side door, shoulders squared, walking straight into the storm—where voices carried and tensions thickened.

"I'll say it one more time, real slow-like so's ya understand. Will an' Gid Crockett are fugitives wanted for murder back in Clarendon. Don't know what they told ya, but they're liars and killers both. If ya know what's good fer ya, send 'em out, an' we'll be on our way."

Rounding the corner of the house, Will and Gid saw Martha step forward, chin held high, jaw set firm as a bear trap.

"What's good for us? Now you listen here. Take your men and your guns and remove yourselves from my property this instant. We will *not* succumb to intimidation, even if you are wearing a badge. That may be your mark in society, but out here, it's what's behind the badge that counts, not what a man wears on his hip or spits from his mouth."

"Madam, I ain't got the time nor the patience ta deal with an ornery woman." Wolfe shifted in his saddle, noticeably irritated.

"Now that ain't a proper way ta speak ta a lady, Mr. Wolfe," Gid said, walking next to Will as they approached the sheriff from his blind side.

Scanning the scene, Will noted sudden movement near the front window, then saw Jack next to Martha on the porch with the rest of the Triple Bar S crew crowding closely behind as he slid his thumb to his gun belt. His eyes darted to the riders just in time to see the deputies reach for their pistols.

"Wouldn't do that if I were you." Will's shout

snapped heads his way. The deputies yanked their sidearms. He threw up his hand, palm out, stopping them cold, and pointed.

"You can't see from where you're sitting, but there's a rifle in the window pointed at your head. Not sure which of you is in its sight. I'll leave that for you to decide."

Will lowered his hand, but the deputies did not lower their weapons. Wolfe scowled.

"Yer puttin' these folks in danger, Mr. Crockett. You an' yer brother, that is, just like ya did back at Cletus's cabin." Wolfe leaned forward. He glowered, smug as a rattler coiled and basking under the sun, ignoring the warning and dismissing the crowd on the porch. "It's a good thing what's left of his family made the train ta Amarillo yesterday, like the widow informed me. Safe an' sound by now, I reckon. Far away from the both of ya."

"Ya know the one thing that's the same 'bout men like yerself, Mr. Wolfe?"

"Sheriff Wolfe," he stammered. "It's best ya remember that."

"Lemme tell ya, Mr. Wolfe," Gid continued, unfazed. "Men like y'all have no idea when you've crossed the line. Y'ave stepped over it so many times, it's hard ta tell where the law ends and corruption begins. It's like there ain't a line a'tall."

A tense silence hung between them, thick as heat before the approaching storm. The deputies, still gripping their pistols, exchanged wary glances.

Like sturdy oaks rooted deep in the earth, Will and Gid did not budge. Will kept his hand close to his own gun, watching the way their fingers twitched, the way they shifted in their saddles. Every man here could sense it—one wrong move, one nervous trigger finger, and the whole thing would explode.

Wolfe sneered, his fingers tightening around the reins. "Ain't no lawman in the territory gonna take kindly ta a couple a drifters threatenin' the badge."

Gid exhaled slowly and deliberately, his jaw tightening. "Ain't no lawman worth his badge oughta be threatenin' women and children neither."

Martha stepped forward then, her hands clenched at her sides. "Sheriff, you best ride outta here while you still have the chance."

Wolfe shifted his attention to her, his lip curling. "You talk awful big standin' behind a wall of men."

"The only ones here behind something is your men and their guns," Martha shot back. "But you, Sheriff Wolfe, got plenty to hide behind? I can tell when a man is lying, when he's thought to have gained the upper hand by the stories he claims as truth. Maybe that's why you're so eager to arrest these men. You're afraid that they may reveal more than you are willing to claim."

The words hit like a branding iron. Wolfe's face hardened, his eyes narrowing to slits. Deputies Withers and McGraw exchanged uneasy glances. Edgar Hunt froze, wide-eyed and silent.

Wolfe sneered, ignoring the tension. "The only truth here, madam, is that Will and Gid Crockett are killers."

"Yer a liar!" Henry's voice rose above the rest as he forced his way past the mob of cowboys surrounding Martha. Before he could leap off the porch, she grabbed him by the shoulders and held him back.

"I heard ya, Sheriff! Heard ya both plannin' ta go after Will an' Gid, but if ya couldn't find 'em, ya said you'd go after my ma, blame her for them dead men. The *sheriff's* men. Ain't that right, Mr. Hunt?"

"Well, I'll be. Buster...that you? This ain't the time ta be spreadin' more lies, son," Hunt said, his voice shaky.

"I ain't lyin'. An' I ain't yer son. I heard ya in the livery talkin'. The sheriff sent those men ta the cabin after Pa was shot." He turned his attention to Wolfe. "Now that they're dead, yer not out fer justice. Yer huntin' fer blood."

Wolfe turned to look at Hunt. Hunt stared back at him, his slack-jawed, guilt-stricken expression crumbling into panic as all eyes turned on him.

"Damn, Edgar. Seems as if yer barn is crawlin' with rats."

In one swift, fluid motion, Wolfe drew his pistol and aimed at Hunt.

BANG!

The shot boomed out, sudden and merciless. Hunt's head snapped back, blood bursting from the clean hole in his forehead as he toppled backward off his horse. His lifeless body hit the dirt with a dull thud, dust puffing around him.

Wolfe's revolver swung next, straight toward Henry.

"NO!" Martha shrieked.

But before Wolfe could fire, Jack's sidearm roared. The bullet slammed into Wolfe's shoulder, ripping him backward from his saddle. His pistol fired wild, the round slicing harmlessly into the sky as he crashed to the ground, groaning in pain.

The pause didn't last.

The deputies opened fire.

Will dove left, landing hard on his side, dust biting at his teeth. His gun cleared leather in a heartbeat, the first shot catching a deputy's hat and knocking it clean off. The crack of gunfire sent the horses into a frenzy. Withers lost his grip and tumbled from the saddle. Will fired again, his shot punching into the dirt inches from McGraw's boot, making the man jolt sideways and scramble for cover.

Gid was already moving. He barreled forward, low and fast, bullets snapping past his ears. One skimmed the dust at his feet. Another splintered a fence post behind him. But Gid didn't flinch. He rammed his shoulder into McGraw's horse, spooking it sideways, and grabbed the deputy by his coat.

With a grunt, Gid ripped McGraw clean off the saddle. They crashed into the dirt in a tangled heap of fists and boots. McGraw swung first, catching Gid across the jaw, but Gid barely felt it. He jabbed the man in the ribs, then again in the face, blood spraying as McGraw's nose broke under the force.

Meanwhile, Will kept firing.

A round zinged past his temple. Will rolled onto his stomach and sighted the second deputy. Withers ducked behind a corral post, then leaned out to fire.

Before he could squeeze the trigger, a rifle shot boomed from the house.

BLAM!

Withers screamed, his leg buckling beneath him as Stanton's bullet found its mark. He tumbled into the dirt, clutching his thigh, blood pooling fast.

Will shot a glance toward the window. Stanton met his gaze, nodding.

A hard whump of fists hitting flesh pulled Will's attention back to Gid. The two men were rolling in the dirt, Gid landing heavy punches even as McGraw clawed for a boot knife. Seeing it, Gid twisted, elbowed McGraw in the throat, and yanked the blade away.

"Ya done?" Gid growled.

McGraw swung a wild punch at Gid's waist.

"Didn't think so."

Gid reared back and slammed the hilt of the knife into McGraw's ear, knocking him cold.

The air thickened with the smell of gunpowder. Bodies groaned on the ground. Withers clutched his leg, McGraw lay unconscious, and Wolfe struggled to crawl backward, his wounded shoulder hanging limp.

A beat of silence preceded the soft hum of heavy mist drifting in—light at first before thickening—coating the dust and mingling with spilled blood. Will stood, boots flecked with fresh mud forming in the churned-up dirt. He locked eyes on Wolfe and stepped forward.

"Y-you...you're gonna hang for this," Wolfe spat, blood slicking his chin.

Will leveled his gun at the man's head. "You first."

The rain picked up. Thunder growled low on the horizon, distant but rolling in.

Gid stepped up beside Will, wiping a smear of blood from his jawline. "Ain't no one left to back yer lies now, Sheriff."

The Triple Bar S hands spread out, guns still raised but lowering slowly, the storm washing over them. Jack holstered his pistol, his jaw tight as he looked at the bodies.

"Y'all sure know how to bring hell with ya, mates," he muttered.

Will shrugged, holstering his weapon. "Storms don't come quiet."

The drizzle thickened into a steady downpour, hammering the dirt and washing blood into the mud. Gid looked up through the cleansing sheets.

"Helluva day."

Will nodded. "Ain't over yet."

CHAPTER FORTY-EIGHT

"WELL, LOOKIE LOOKIE, TATER. SEE ALL THEM WOOD crosses scattered 'round with names carved in 'em? An' look there, ya can see the ground ain't even, like more bodies are buried deep down, but nothin' above sayin' who they was or how they got dead. I kinda like that." Sully sat on his horse, looking over the rough-plank fence of Tascosa's Boot Hill cemetery, and smiled. "When I die, that's what I want. Don't need no one lookin' down on me. Pityin' me. Wonderin' if I'm floatin' in heaven or burnin' in hell. Nope. Ta hell with 'em all." Turning to Tater, his smile widened, carving deep lines in his face like a ripe jack-o'-lantern. "What'd ya think? That how you wanna go?"

Tater stared at the bare-bones graves, his eyes focusing on a wilted bushel of dried flowers slumped against a rotten stake beneath its cross. He whispered his reply. "I ain't ready ta die yet."

Sully leaned in, cupping a dirty hand behind his ear. "Speak up. I cain't hear ya, dummy. Ya want that, too?"

Tater turned his head slowly, his gaze sweeping over

the crooked crosses before meeting Sully's distant glare and wide, jagged grin. "I said, I ain't ready ta die yet, Sully. Anyhow, when I'm gone, ain't no one gonna be around ta make that kind of decision fer me."

Sully's smile disappeared, replaced by a sarcastically confused look. "What d'ya mean? I'll be around." Leaning forward, Sully hawked over the fence, his glob of spit landing just short of a freshly staked pine cross. "Damn. Missed." Still gazing at the poor-man's graveyard, Sully nodded as if he had come to an agreeable conclusion about their conversation. "Don't ya worry one bit, little brother. I won't let anyone mark yer grave so's they can judge ya, neither. It'll be like we never existed a'tall."

Sully yanked the reins, pulling his horse away from the fence.

"C'mon. We'll git us a room at the Stone Hotel, then head downstairs ta the saloon fer a drink, courtesy of our flyin' friends back at camp."

Tater paused, then looked beyond the graveyard at the small town of Tascosa. He could see the hotel towering above the rest of the buildings, remembering the last time they were there. When they lost everything they had, making honest bets but outsmarted by fast-talking Faro dealers.

"We shouldn't be here," he said, speaking to the dead at his feet. Looking across the uneven bulges, he landed on a flat patch of land near the opposite side of the cemetery. Sully's horse ambled just beyond the fence, and for an instant, what Tater saw, or thought he saw, was unexplainable—like the ground had opened, and Sully willingly rode straight into its gaping black hole.

Tater smacked the side of his head with his palm.

"Don't go losin' yer wits, Tater," he mumbled. "Ya've already lost yer nerve."

Hearing a sharp whistle, Tater looked to see Sully waving him ahead and already sensed his growing agitation.

As he rode to catch up to his crazed brother, he felt the pull of Boot Hill behind him, its lonely call beckoning him to make a swift and more permanent return.

CHAPTER FORTY-NINE

Rain poured over the ranch, washing away spilled blood and the foul scent of gunfire and fighting men, but like the battle, it did not last. It swept over the land like a rogue wave, turning dry earth to mud and leaving a hiss in the air as the sun burned through its humid wake. Before it was over, Will, Gid, Jack, and a handful of Triple Bar S hands overpowered Sheriff Wolfe and his deputies, dragging them into the barn and tying them to the sturdy posts inside. The prisoners had been lucky. Their injuries were not life-threatening, but the sting of defeat was etched across their hardened scowls.

"This ain't over," Wolfe said as Will checked the knotted rope behind him. "Ya don't have any idea who I am."

Will stepped around Wolfe and was joined by Gid and Jack.

"I don't give a damn who you are, Wolfe," Will said, his jaw tight. "Only thing that matters to me is what you've done and who you did it to."

Gid stepped forward. "I'd be willin' to bet the Texas

Rangers see it the same way. Ain't nobody above the law, Mr. Wolfe."

"Sheriff Wolfe!" His voice echoed through the rafters, but his tone fell on deaf ears.

"Not for long, mate," Jack said. "Sit tight, all right? Won't be too long before I git back from Amarillo with a real lawman. Ya can spill yer guts ta him when he takes ya up ta the Potter County Jail."

"Amarillo," Gid said, turning to Will and Jack. "Ain't that where he said Liza an' the kids were headed? Shoot. Rangers don't need ta hear the story from us. Once we git Henry back with his family, they can all tell the tale of how ya ruined their lives." Gid's tone sharpened as he directed his attention to Wolfe. "Stompin' on their pa's grave like ya did."

Will grabbed Gid's shoulder, firm but calm. It was enough to hold him back—barely.

"I think what my brother is trying to say is that your days are numbered, Wolfe."

Gid straightened, his breath heavy, until Jack patted his arm and pointed to the barn door.

Randall entered the barn with a satchel slung over his shoulder, gripping Edgar Hunt's lifeless arms while another ranch hand held his feet. They hauled Hunt to an empty stall at the back, dumping him inside before Randall rejoined the men gathered around Wolfe.

"Looks like yer gonna git patched up. Try an' be a good patient," Jack said.

"I ain't nobody's patient," Wolfe sneered.

"That's all right, mate. Randall ain't really a doctor."

Will, Gid, and Jack turned and walked out of the barn, leaving Randall to deal with the grumbling Wolfe and his miscreant deputies. Martha was waiting for them at the top of the porch.

"It's settled, then? Jack will accompany you to Tascosa, help apprehend the murderers, and then return here with the rangers to claim the scoundrels in my barn?"

"I think that's a plan we can live with, Mrs. Wilson," Will said.

"What about the boy?" she asked. "I think it would be best if he remain here. It's far too dangerous for him to ride along."

"Well, ma'am, that's not a half-bad idea," Gid said.

"Yes it is!" Henry rushed through the front door, stopping at the top of the steps. "I'm goin' with ya," he said, chest heaving with determination.

"Ya been listenin', Henry?" Gid said.

"Yes, sir."

"Seems like there ain't a conversation ta be had without ya knowin' somethin' about it. But, Mrs. Wilson is right. We ain't just strollin' through town. Tascosa is a rough place, with men just as bad as the ones we're after."

"But I'm the only one who knows their voices. I bet there's a ton of men with the same name, but I can't git their voices outta my head. That should be good fer somethin'."

Will and Gid shared a glance.

"You know, Will. Henry was brave enough ta go it alone just ta find us. May have been a risk he shouldn't have taken, but he did, an' here we are. Ya might say Henry saved our lives. I don't think we can leave 'im outta this one."

Will turned to Henry. "Get your gear in order. We leave within the hour."

Henry shook his head, then jumped from the stoop into the thin mud and raced to the stables.

"The kid's got gumption," Jack said.

"Try not to get him killed, Mr. Crockett?" Martha said, concern woven into her voice and reflected in her gaze.

"Oh, Henry'll be all right," Gid said. "Don't you worry, Mrs. Wilson."

Pursing her lips, Martha folded her hands. "I suppose there's no talking you into taking more of my men?"

Will shook his head, his eyes flicking from Jack to Gid before settling on Martha. "More men will only attract more attention. If the killers are still in Tascosa, we don't want to give them reason to bolt if word gets around that we're looking for them."

"Very well, Mr. Crockett."

"Please, call me Will."

Martha sighed. "Jack. Do be careful. And come back with the rangers as soon as you can."

He tipped his hat, replying as she returned to the house. "Yes, ma'am." Standing with Will and Gid, the three men looked north, Jack nodded. "Should reach town by nightfall, long as we don't run into any further unexpected trouble."

"A-yuh," Will and Gid replied in unison.

Will added. "We'll have plenty...once we knock on the devil's door."

CHAPTER FIFTY

THE SUN SANK IN THE WESTERN SKY AS WILL, GID, Henry, and Jack crossed the Canadian River, their shadows growing longer as they approached Tascosa. Entering at the west end of town, Main Street opened before them, stretching wide past bustling boardwalks and lively saloons. The sight caused Henry's jaw to drop.

"It's a sight, ain't it, Henry?" Jack said, noticing the boy's wonder.

"It sure is, but why are the buildings so far apart?"

"Tascosa is a cow town. Ranches like the Triple Bar S drive their cattle through on their way to the Chisholm Trail. The buildings were built far across from each other so that herds of cattle could be brought straight through town."

A dull haze settled in as the sun dipped lower, its bottom kissing the horizon with a distant sizzle. Cowboys milled about, each eyeing the riders as they passed. Walking along the edge of the dusty road, a lamplighter tended to lanterns lining the street, ensuring each one was lit as dusk fell over the town.

Henry squinted, looking one way, then another. "Where do you think they are, Gid?"

"Good question, Henry," Gid said, scanning groups of men they rode past. "Could be anywhere, so keep yer voice down."

"That's right, Henry. We must be careful," Will added. "There are ears everywhere."

Henry looked from side to side. "Ears?"

Jack leaned in. "It means people ya don't see might be listenin'."

"Right," Gid agreed.

"First things first," Will said. "Let's find a place to hole up for the night, then regroup and start our search."

"Why don't y'all head over to the Stone Hotel?" Jack said. "I'll go see the marshal about contacting the Texas Rangers and meet you there."

"Be careful," Will said. "You hear the names Sully or Tater, that'll be our guys. Come find us and we'll take 'em together."

With a nod, Jack broke off from the group. Will, Henry, and Gid continued along Main Street, pulling up to a hitching post in front of the hotel. Will and Gid hopped off their horses. Henry remained in the saddle, still mesmerized by the strange, new town.

"You okay, Henry?" Gid asked.

"It's just different from Clarendon. I ain't never traveled nowhere before."

"Believe me, there's a lot more to the world than what yer seein' right here, Henry."

"I bet. Ya think I'll see it one day?"

Looping the reins of his horse around the post, Gid replied. "What?"

"The world."

Henry studied the drifting sea of cowboys, his gaze skimming past finely dressed women standing beside men in glasses and suits.

"Hop on down, Henry," Will said. "Let's all go inside together."

Handing Will the reins, Henry slid out of the saddle, the thump of his boots muffled by a sudden roar of celebratory laughter from inside the saloon. He jerked his head toward the batwings, curiosity tugging at him as he stepped onto the boardwalk.

"Don't go wandering off," Will warned. He glanced up and down the wooden walkway, catching tightened glares and wandering eyes from strangers lingering nearby. "There are some unsavory-looking characters around."

With the horses secured at the hitching post, Gid and Henry followed Will into the Stone Hotel's main lobby.

A large circular wrought iron chandelier hung from the center of the ceiling. Twelve candles stood at attention around the rustic perimeter, their flaming hats dancing in the subtle drafts drifting through the building. Stationed to the left—and along the wall opposite the saloon entrance—was an elegant, wooden registration counter. A short man wearing a black vest with purple trim stood behind it, waiting to engage his next guest.

"Howdy, friends. My name's Eugene Wallace. Welcome to the Stone Hotel," he said as Will, Gid, and Henry approached. "Couple rooms for the gentlemen?"

Will placed a hand on the counter and leaned forward. "We'll take one room. Largest available."

The clerk's eyes flicked to Henry. "This your son, mister?"

"Nephew," Gid said, stepping in. "The boy said he wanted ta see the world. His ma said ridin' with us might just put some hair on his chest." Gid slapped Henry's back, causing him to jostle.

"I suppose it could," the clerk replied, then looked at Henry, "Where ya off to next, son?"

"Our room, Mr. Wallace, if you please," Will said, cutting the inquiry short.

Squinting one eye above a souring smile, the clerk reached below the counter and produced a room key, showing it to Will. "Room 6, second floor." His welcoming charm turned curt. "Bath's down the hall." He set it on the countertop, but before Will could take the key, the clerk looked past him, blossomed a fresh smile, and greeted a young couple walking into the lobby from the street.

"Welcome. Welcome, my friends," he said, stepping out from behind the counter and leaving Will and the rest standing alone. His voice rebounded with graciousness, captivating the couple with false charm.

"Friendly, 'til he ain't," Gid said.

Will snatched the key. "Come on, let's find the room, then head down for a bite and wait for Jack."

"Now, that's the best idea I've heard all day, Will," Gid said as they made their way across the lobby to the stairs.

Henry lingered, stealing a glance into the saloon before following the others up the stairs. The clinking of ivory keys and bursts of festive chatter filled the room. Its blend of conversations, undulating cheers, and the occasional blurt of belly laughter appealed to

Henry, but the smell of hot food wafting from the kitchen made the biggest impact, causing his stomach to growl.

As he gazed into the crowded saloon, he noticed a group of tables surrounded by men along the far wall, each man engaged with someone sitting on the other side. He saw paper bills clenched in fists, scowls mixed with smiles, and bobbing heads, some with slicked hair, others wearing fancy hats. "Sake's alive," he muttered.

"Henry," Will called halfway up the stairs.

Henry turned to catch up, climbing the stairs but looking over his shoulder. His mind was still fixed on a favorite hat among the group. A rounded black bowler caught his eye, as did a high-crowned Gus-style, but the one that held his attention most was a felt hat with a fancy feather.

CHAPTER FIFTY-ONE

NEAR THE FARO TABLES, THE JINGLE OF COINS AND THE whisp of folded bills landing on felt excited Sully. With hands in his pockets, he fingered his filthy lucre, money stolen from the corpses and profits made from selling the supplies he and Tater hauled into town, but he resisted the temptation to gamble. In his blackened core, he had other reasons for being here, none of which required money. Bullets were his currency, and his winnings would be dragged through blood.

Next to him, Tater fidgeted, leaning one way, then the other, trying to get a clear look at the table to watch the action.

Biting down on his tongue, Tater watched as the next turn began. After the dealer finalized the bets, he slid the top card from a Faro shoe, revealing the queen of spades, the banker's card. A collective groan rippled through the table as losing bets were swept away. The dealer slid his hand to the Faro shoe and glanced at the gamblers across the table.

"C'mon, dealer," one man pleaded. "Anythin' but a queen."

"Good luck to ya, friend," the dealer said, sliding the next card across the table, this time flipping a second queen. "No joy, partner."

A second round of disappointed grunts and groans came, some muttered curses tangled between them, as the house claimed all bets on a double.

"Son of a bitch!" another irate gambler said. "You knew'd what was comin', didn't ya?"

Ignoring the man, the dealer looked around the huddled card players. "New deal comin'. Make your play or sit it out."

Leaning close to Sully, Tater whispered. "That's how we lost, remember?"

Flaring his nostrils and clenching his jaw, Sully's eyes darted from the dealer to the angry gambler. Sensing the hostility, he whispered back, "This turn ain't over yet."

Still fuming over the loss, the gambler's rant carried over the table. "Goddamn queen! Yer cheatin'. Don't know how, but ya are! I outta—" His hand dropped toward his belt, but before he could blink, he froze. Two sawed-off barrels pressed under his nose as the casekeeper working next to the dealer stared down the sights without so much as a twitch.

Tater retreated, as did the other players standing around the table. All except the man eating the shotgun barrel, and Sully.

"Go ahead," the casekeeper said. "Skin that weapon if ya like."

Sully felt a cool twinge in his spine, as if ice water had dripped down his back. Watching the scene unfold was like inhaling the trapped vapors from a fresh bottle of aged whiskey, uncorked and breathing only for him, except he was not afforded the smooth burn of the first sip. It gnawed at him. He wanted to drink, to experience the rush. To feel the power.

"May want ta step back, friend," the dealer said to Sully. "Things might get a bit messy."

Fixed on the casekeeper and the hungry shotgun, Sully ignored the dealer's remarks.

Standing well behind the action, Tater crept forward and tugged Sully's arm. "The man said ta lookout."

Sully yanked his arm back but did not move.

"If ya can't handle the heat," the casekeeper said, pressing the barrel further into the gambler's skin, "ain't no use carryin' a hog like that. Slide it over. Slowly."

The gambler swallowed, then reluctantly lifted his pistol from his belt and placed it on the table. The dealer grabbed the gun, gave it a glance, then tucked it away under the table.

Tater slunk backward, melting into the crowd, as the casekeeper rounded the table and escorted the disgraced gambler out the backdoor of the saloon at gunpoint. Sully watched and grinned, catching the attention of the dealer.

"Somethin' amusing about what happened, friend?"

Cocking his head, Sully spoke as he watched the casekeeper return to the table, noticing a fresh splash of blood dripping from the stock of his gun. "Dumbass move if'n ya ask me."

Not waiting for a reply, Sully spun around and walked past Tater.

"C'mon dummy. Yer gonna need some energy fer what I got planned. Let's eat."

Tater trailed behind, nearly stumbling when Sully stopped short. Sully turned, his gaze locking onto his brother's haunted eyes, latching on to the fear he saw swimming behind them. If weighted pockets equaled heavy hearts, Tater was the lead-bearing mule, and Sully his master.

"Order whatever ya like, Tater. Last meal's on me."

CHAPTER FIFTY-TWO

THE WOODEN STAIRCASE CREAKED AS WILL, GID, AND Henry descended into the lobby, fresh from a quick stop in their room.

"Either of you see Jack?" Will asked.

Gid stepped outside for a look. Henry peeked into the saloon but did not see him. After a second glance, he looked back at Will, shaking his head.

Will stepped up beside Henry, scanning the saloon himself before pointing to an empty table against the far wall.

"Gid and I will grab a seat inside. I want you to stay here until Jack shows."

"But you said—"

"You'll be fine. We'll be able to see you the whole time. I'll order up some food. If Jack doesn't show by the time it arrives, you can join us and eat."

"Okay," Henry said.

A moment later, Gid walked through the hotel entrance alone.

"Jack ain't anywhere as far as I can see," he said, joining Will and Henry.

"He'll show up sooner or later," Will replied. "Henry's gonna hang here and keep lookout."

Gid glanced at Henry.

"Payin' yer dues, eh Henry?"

"I wanna catch"—Henry looked around, checking for eavesdroppers, then lowered his voice—"you know who, just as much as y'all."

"Well, with you standin' guard, we got a pretty good chance," Gid said. "Hang tight. Jack'll be along soon."

Will and Gid made their way through the saloon to the empty table and took a seat while Henry leaned against the door frame between the Stone Hotel lobby and the saloon entrance and waited.

Will surveyed the room: the active Faro tables, a six-man game of five-card-stud, cowboys at the bar with their boots hooked on the brass footrail, and tables with men and women drinking, eating, and swapping stories—until his gaze landed on a petite redhead sauntering their way.

"Howdy, boys. In the mood for something hot and wet?"

Gid and Will exchanged a glance. The girl could not have been older than twenty, but the way she carried herself said she was already a pro.

"If ya mean a well-done steak an' a beer, I'd be happier than a horse in high clover," Gid said with a grin.

Flaunting her hips, she turned to Will. "What about you, mister?"

"Oh, I'll have the same. In fact, make it three servings in all... except for the beer. Just two of those."

The girl twitched her lips to one side. "Three steaks and two beers? Nothin' else ya see that ya like?"

Smiling, Will replied, "What's your name, miss?"

"The name's Candy. I'm sweet as a whistle and I'll melt in your mouth."

Will folded his hands on the table and looked up at Candy. "Just the food."

"An' the beer," Gid added.

Rolling her eyes, Candy spun around and walked away, disappearing through a door where a tinge of smoke and a satisfying helping of delicious aromas wafted out.

"She looks more about like Henry's age, don't ya think, Will?"

"A-yuh. Too bad, too. Reminds me of Anna. Hope she and Scooter are on top of things back at the Brown Spur."

"Think we'll ever get back to the ranch?"

"Maybe. But didn't you say we were headed for the Pacific coast? Could be years before we set foot in this neck of the woods again."

"It's true, ain't it. Settlin' down just ain't in our bones, Will."

"I'll drink to that."

"Soon as we have those beers, ya can."

Gid glanced at Henry. "That boy over there's gonna have a tough life ahead of him."

Will nodded. "Oh, I don't know. It's tragic what happened to his pa, but it may have been a blessing in disguise. If he were still around, Henry may be in more danger than what he is in today."

"I s'pose," Gid said, leaning back on two legs of his

chair. "Let's just make sure he an' his ma are settled before we head out."

The click of glass on the table and the slosh of head spilling over its rim interrupted their conversation.

"Two beers like ya asked for. Steaks'll take some time."

"Thank you, Candy," Will said.

Leaning closer to Will, her perfume added a scent of roses to mix with the smoke and beer. "If either of you change your mind about having a little company, I'll be right over there." She pressed a finger to her lips, then pointed to a stool at the bar before twirling around and walking away, her sway attracting more eyes than just Will and Gid's.

———

HENRY SHIFTED his gaze between the saloon and the front door, boredom creeping in as his stomach rumbled. Watching Will and Gid sip their beers and catching a hint of fresh food beneath the smoky saloon air only made his hunger worse. Where was Jack? He was told to stay in sight, but a flicker of light outside the front door attracted his attention.

I'll just take a quick peek, look for Jack, and see what's going on, he thought.

Quick on his feet, he slipped through the door onto the boardwalk. The light came from torches in the hands of two men on horseback, both swearing at one another while men on the street gathered around.

"What are they doing?" he said to himself, not realizing his voice carried.

"They're fixin' ta race, kid," a man nearby said.

"They carry the torches so's we can see how far they've gone an' when they're headed back." The man continued to talk, but his voice blurred, swelling in Henry's ears like a whirring echo. His hands began to shake. A warm urge pressed into his gut. Voices loomed, but the ringing in Henry's ears sounded like church bells. On weakened knees, he turned for the door, accidentally bumping into another man exiting the hotel.

"What the hell?" he said, shoving Henry to the side.

Startled, Henry first looked at the man's face, then his eyes lifted to the fancy hat with a feather tucked in the band. He opened his mouth but no words came out. The man tilted his head and leaned over him.

"What's wrong with ya, boy? Ya look like ya've seen a ghost."

Scrambling, Henry bolted for the entrance, but the man caught him by the collar before he could get away.

"I said, what's the matter, kid? Ain't polite runin' off without answerin'."

"Aww, let 'im go, Sully."

Henry's eyes bulged. The warmth in his gut unleashed a frightened drizzle down his leg.

"Shit! Ya gonna piss yerself right here?"

"The man said, let him go." Through all the commotion, the Australian twang was music to Henry's ears. "Now I'm tellin' ya ta do the same, mate."

Lynching Henry's collar tighter, Sully spun him around. Standing in the street and glaring at them was Jack.

With his free hand, Sully reached behind his back and removed a Green River Skinner, a blade found among the supplies at the canyon camp, and held it close to Henry's side. "Or what?"

Behind Jack, the crowd roared as the horse race began. Flames soared along the darkened street like devilish flags flapping behind a pair of ghost riders. Drifting away from the front of the hotel as if caught in an undertow, the crowd followed the fiery trail, shouting and whooping into the shadows of Tascosa, leaving Jack squared off with Sully, Henry under his lethal control.

"What are ya doin', Sully?"

"Shut it, Tater. This boy wronged me, an' now he's gonna pay the price."

Sully looked around, spotting an alleyway beside the saloon. Slowly, with Henry in his grasp and knife still pressed against him, he moved along the boardwalk to the edge of the building.

"Damn, Sully. Not like this." Tater said, his voice stretching.

"I said shut up!"

What men and women were outside were more interested in the race and their potential purse and did not see what was happening so close to them.

"Sully. Yer Sully?" Jack said, keeping his distance but matching him step for step.

"What of it?"

"Yer the ones that killed my friends and my boss." Jack clenched his fists. "And ya killed the boy's father, too."

Stepping in front of Jack, Tater stared at Sully. "That can't be, can it?"

Sully snarled. He bared teeth before yelling at his brother. "You ain't never gonna learn, dummy."

"Let the boy go, Sully." Tater pleaded. "I ain't gonna let ya kill another innocent. Especially not no child."

"What are you? God? Ain't no such thing, or we'd

never been as bad off as we were. Now we got money. Power. An' it's only gonna git better. Maybe not fer you, Tater. But fer me, the sky's the limit."

"No," Tater said, his voice dropping to a whisper. Then again, "No!"

He yelled loud enough to draw the attention of people down the street and inside the hotel. Tater's one word climbed the mountain that was Sully's delirium, cutting straight to his core, but all Sully did was curl his lips into an evil, dissolute grin. "Say goodbye ta the boy."

Moving as if lighting shot from his legs, Tater bolted at Sully, charging him with a war cry born from desperation. "AHHHHH!"

Sully watched Tater shoot toward him. In disbelief, he flinched, pulling the knife away from Henry's body. Henry felt the give, raised his boot, and stomped down hard on Sully's foot. The jarring, solid heel caused enough pain that Sully loosened his grip, allowing Henry to wriggle free just before Tater rammed into Sully.

Henry fell to the side.

Sully and Tater tumbled to the boardwalk.

A woman exiting the hotel was startled by the fight and screamed, which caused a flood of people to rush out the door to see what was happening.

Jack ran to Henry, scooped him up, and pulled him safely away from the scrum in which Tater and Sully were entangled.

Fists flew. Wood rattled under their bodies as they rolled to the edge of the boardwalk and into the street. Their bodies landed with a thud.

Will and Gid hurried out the door and pushed their

way through the growing crowd, locating Jack and Henry.

"What the hell happened?" Will said.

"It's them," Henry replied, pointing. "It's Tater an' Sully. The men who killed my pa."

Gid and Will turned to see the jumble of men fighting, then heard the wail of a high-pitched scream rise from their mess. The tussle came to a sudden halt.

Sully rolled away from Tater, his knife and hands covered with blood. He glared at Henry, at the crowd, his audience, slowly drawing his mouth open to show teeth. "I tol' the dummy to keep quiet. Y'all heard me." Jumping to his feet, he ran into the alley.

"Stay here, Henry," Gid ordered as he and Will ran after Sully.

Jack and two other men watching ran to Tater. Henry followed at a distance, wanting to see, yet not wanting to at all.

Blood spilled into the dirt from a puncture wound in Tater's side and another between his ribs closer to the center of his chest.

Jack approached with caution, then leaned over Tater and rolled him onto his back.

Tater coughed and wheezed, each time spitting globs of blood from his mouth, but he did not try to move. He lay in the dirt, feeling his body throb with each beat of his heart, and cried.

It was not pain that caused his tears to flow.

It was relief.

CHAPTER FIFTY-THREE

THE ALLEY WAS LONG AND DARK, A SHADOWED TUNNEL alive with rapid footsteps and sharp cries. Dusk had reached its deepest point, the sky a blooming blackness where vibrant stars flickered to life, scattered above like fireflies over the Canadian River. The smell of burning meat from the kitchen seeped through the porous walls of the Stone Saloon, drifting in the secluded air like the foul fumes of cannon smoke after a deadly blast. Racing through it all, Will and Gid chased Sully, their boots pounding as the noise from the street behind them faded into the night.

Instead of opening at the rear of the saloon, the alley cut sharply right, narrowing into a tighter passage that ran between an adjacent building and the remnants of a dilapidated livery. Breathing heavily but relishing the thrill of his escape, Sully barreled ahead until he spotted a thin shred of light shining through a gap in the crumbling stable wall. Sliding to a stop, he looked over his shoulder and saw two blackened forms closing in fast. His gaze flicked back to the glowing gap, then to his pursuers. A wicked grin spread across his face.

"Yer playin' with the devil, boys," he called out, his voice laced with lunacy. "Come join me in hell."

His invitation echoed between the buildings, lingering in the dead air before he ducked into the maze of rotten stables.

———

HEARING SULLY'S WORDS, Will slowed his pace, reaching out his arms to stop Gid.

"Hear him? Sounds crazier than a preacher at a poker game," Will said.

Swaying and ready for anything, Gid eyed the point in the wall where Sully disappeared. "We goin' in, or what?"

Will pulled his pistol. "I bring the fire. You bring the fury."

"An' the devil will eat our lead," Gid said, drawing his weapon.

The brothers exchanged a nod, then, one by one, slipped through the splintering timber.

Light from a single lantern hanging at the far end of the open-air building burned bright enough to fill the stables with golden light. It also created bottomless shadows, any of which could conceal a man. The space was quiet, the stillness amplifying the weight of ambush or surprise.

Will and Gid spread out, weaving through the stable's crisscrossing halls, eyes sweeping over fallen boards and rotted stalls, tracking every shadow. Their gazes flicked up to the rafters, then back over their shoulders, covering their tracks.

With guns held low and tight, fingers hovering just outside the trigger, they pressed on, bravery and instinct guiding them, as it had their entire lives.

Will moved around a pile of rafter wood where a section of the roof had collapsed. Gid ducked through an open stall, stepping over the dividing planks of its broken wall and exiting into the walkway on the other side, all the while staying within sight of one another.

Rising from the depths of the structure, a wicked cackle broke the silence. Words followed, but their meanings were incomprehensible, twisted, and senseless, yet flowed with poetic cadence.

"Ain't no dogs gonna bite. Ain't no bees stingin' me. Ain't no end in sight. An' yer dyin' ain't free."

Raising his gun higher and motioning toward the voice, Will steadied his aim. "There's no need for anyone else to die, Sully."

Gid crouched low and crept forward.

Will watched and kept talking. "Y'all killed the boy's pa over in Clarendon. And the men just south of here. Now, the man you were tusslin' with is likely dyin' in the street right now."

"Tater? Dyin'?" Sully's voice edged higher, thick with something between disbelief and amusement. "He always was a dummy. Gone an' got hisself killed, an' fer what?"

Gid quickened his pace, flanking the spot where Sully's voice snaked through the stables.

"He's dyin' because of you, Sully," Will said. "Your knife. Your hands."

A pause rippled between them, followed by chatter as if Sully was talking to himself.

"My hands 're red. My knife is, too. Tater's dead, on account of you."

Piercing laughter burst from the stall where Sully was hiding, growing enraged and filling the air. With guns drawn, he stood and thrust them in front of him, each barrel erupting with deadly force.

Will dove to the side, crashing through a brittle wooden wall, and landed with a thud in what smelled like an old feed room. Rats scurried along the baseboards, fleeing out the opening to the stalls and into the line of muzzle flashes. Wood splintered as each bullet tore past Will.

From the side, Gid took aim and fired twice at Sully, narrowly missing both shots.

"There ya are," Sully screamed. He turned and fired, but not at Gid. Instead, he aimed at the hayloft directly overhead. Three quick blasts were all it took for the bullets to splinter enough of the rotting support beams for them to crack and crash down.

Gid moved fast, but the falling boards and forgotten, dried bales fell like a rolling wave, crashing down on him before he could get out of the way.

Hearing the crash, Will jumped to his feet and charged out the door. With guns blazing, he fired at Sully. Sully whirled around, mouth stretched wide, taking two of the three shots to his chest.

His body shuddered. His eyes bulged, but his fingers kept working the gun, squeezing the trigger until both cylinders were exhausted.

Dodging the errant shots, Will crashed through the last wooden partition that separated him from Sully like a bull in a stampede, lined his sights, and fired one last shot.

BLAM!

Sully's head snapped back, his eyes rolling upward as if desperate to see the wound. A single stream of blood seeped from the hole in his forehead, tracing a slow path down his face. His body crumpled, dead before he hit the ground, his wicked grin still frozen in place.

Moving quickly, Will lunged past Sully's body, holstering his weapon as he raced to uncover Gid from the fallen rafters and hay.

"Gid. Hold on!"

Piece by piece, Will snatched and threw boards to the side until he saw Gid's fist punch through what was left of the scraps of lumber. Grabbing his hand, he pulled.

"Son of a—" Gid's voice rose with him as Will pulled him clear of the debris. Using both hands to steady his brother, Will looked him in the eye.

"Get a little in over your head, Gid?"

Gid smirked. "No more than usual, Will." Glancing past him, he saw Sully's corpse lying in a heap. "What was he sayin' 'bout dogs an' bees?"

Will laughed, patting Gid on the shoulder. "No telling."

Looking closer, Gid saw Sully's face, then shook his head. "That's about the craziest look I've ever seen on a dead man."

Will shrugged. "The man died how he lived."

Gid paused, then chuckled to himself. "Ain' too sure the devil's gonna like seein' that face fer all eternity."

"Maybe," Will said. "It's not for us to judge, but I bet you're probably right."

CHAPTER FIFTY-FOUR

WILL AND GID MADE THEIR WAY BACK TO THE STREET AND saw that only a handful of onlookers lingered, their curiosity fading. Jack stood with two men wearing badges nearest Tater's body. Approaching the scene, it became clear that Tater was dead. He lay flat on his back, eyes closed, mouth slack, his blood-soaked shirt clinging to his chest. A buckboard rattled to a stop in the middle of the road, drawing the attention of the men talking with Jack. Henry sat on the steps leading to the Stone Hotel, holding a hat with a feather tucked into its band.

"Jack," Will called out.

"Over here, mate." Jack turned to the men wearing badges. "Fellas, this is Will and Gid Crockett. These are the ones I was telling ya 'bout."

"I'm Marshal Seymour Black. This is my deputy, Charlie Coffers," the marshal said, pausing before clicking his tongue and pointing a curious finger at Will and Gid. "Crockett. The name rings a bell."

"Rang many a bell, marshal," Gid replied. "Mostly

good. Other times been misunderstood, but everythin's been straightened out fer years."

"You were in the war?"

"We both were," Will said. "But that's ancient history."

In unison, the men turned their attention to Tater's corpse.

"The boy said this was one of the men that killed his pa. Cletus Morgan, right?" Coffers asked.

Will and Gid nodded.

The marshal added, "Also said he was the one that saved him from getting stabbed. Said he told his brother not to do it. Something like that. Anyway, there he is, killed by a blood relative. Looks like your hunt is over."

"I'd say so," Will said. "The other one, Sully, is lyin' out back. The livery is shot to hell, but it doesn't look like it had much life left before we got there."

"Nope. That place is a hazard," the marshal said. "One spark goes awry, and it could help to burn down the entire town. I'll have the undertaker see to the body after he finishes with this one."

"What about the rangers, Jack?" Will asked.

"Right. Marshal Black'll wire the rangers in the mornin'. I'll hang around town a few days 'til they arrive, then see 'em out to the ranch to collect your beloved sheriff and his men."

The marshal gave a short nod, then he and his deputy walked off to speak to the undertaker.

Gid exhaled through his nose and rolled his shoulders.

Jack smirked as he eyed Gid. "Come on, I'll buy ya both a beer, an' we can put this ta bed."

Will and Gid followed Jack back to the hotel, stopping at the steps next to Henry.

"Ya okay?" Gid asked.

Henry sat staring at the hat in his hands. Hearing Gid's voice, he blinked, then lifted his head. "Yes, sir."

"It's over, Henry," Will said.

"I know." Henry turned to Jack and held out the hat. "Here. I think Mrs. Wilson would want her husband's hat back. This was his, wasn't it?"

Jack smiled at Henry.

"Ya know, she might. But I'd bet she'd rather have someone keep it who'd wear it just as he did. Will ya take care of it for her?"

Henry looked at the hat, gently running his finger along the edge of the feather, then placed it on his head.

"Looks dandy, mate," Jack said.

"Come on, Henry," Gid said, pulling him to his feet. "Let's head inside. Jack's buyin' me an' Will a beer, an' I bet I can find someone ta rustle ya up a piece of pie."

EPILOGUE

THE SUN SAT HIGH IN THE SKY, ITS WARM BEAMS MIXING with a northern breeze. The blend felt refreshing to the touch and naturally delicious with each deep, cleansing breath. The sharp call of a train whistle carried for what seemed like miles on the back of the breeze, announcing its arrival with a fading fluster of steam. Will, Gid, and Henry rode through Amarillo, stopping just short of a little house nestled on the edge of the emerging town.

"Do ya think she'll be mad? Ma, I mean," Henry said, his horse standing between Will and Gid's.

"I bet she'll be more happy ta see ya than anythin' else, Henry," Gid replied.

Flicking the reins, the three urged their horses forward. Each hoof clomp brought Henry closer to his family. It was not quite home, but it was a promise of a fresh start for the Morgans.

As they approached, the front door swung open, and a woman, followed by two girls, ran outside. A second lady followed behind, calmly closing the door behind her.

"Henry?" his mother yelled. "Henry Morgan? Is that you?"

Sliding out of the saddle, Henry tossed the reins to Gid, then ran to his mother.

Joyful tears streamed down Liza's cheeks as she embraced her son, hugging him and silently promising to never let go. His sisters latched onto his sides, smothering him with love.

Will and Gid stayed on their horses. This was not their family. It was not their moment. Both men watched the bonds of a broken family grow stronger by the second, each squeeze, each word reconnecting Henry with his mother and sisters.

Pulling apart but still arm in arm, Liza looked up and saw Will and Gid.

"You brought him back to me."

"Ma'am," Gid started to say, "Liza, you should be mighty proud of that boy. He may have run off like a spring chicken searchin' fer trouble, but me an' Will are alive because of him. There's a lot he's gonna want ta tell ya, an' every bit of it's the truth."

Liza stepped closer to the horses, looking up at both men.

"Thank you," she said. "Thank you for everything you've done for Henry...and for me. I don't know what would have happened if—"

"No, ma'am," Will said softly. "It's us who should be thanking Henry."

Liza squeezed Henry closer, tilting his hat. She smiled, the first real emotion she had reason to reveal in as long as she could remember. She gazed at Gid.

"You can tie up the horses out back. It sure is good to see you both."

Will and Gid exchanged a look.

"Thank you, Liza," Will said. "But me an' Gid will be heading out."

Henry flashed a look at Gid, his face drooping from the sudden news.

"It ain't cause we don't want ta," Gid said. "Y'all have some catchin' up ta do on yer own."

Henry pulled away from his mother.

"Will I ever see ya again?" he said, his eyes darting between the men.

"Shoot, Henry," Gid said. "I don't know why not. Heck, we got ourselves a long-eared rabbit huntin' cabin just south of here I expect ta be visitin' again one of these days."

Liza slipped a laugh, sharing a heartfelt glance with Gid.

Will smiled, then added, "And you can be sure that when we do, we'll swing through and bring you along. Sound good?"

Henry nodded, then stepped between the horses. Looking up, he raised his hand and, one at a time, shook theirs as any man of the house would do.

"Where are ya headed?" he asked, letting go of Gid's hand.

"Well," Gid said. "We were aimin' northwest. I don't see why now would be any different."

"What do ya expect ta see, Gid?" Henry asked, eyes growing large with wonder.

Gid glanced back, the corner of his mouth curling in a knowing smile.

"The world."

IF YOU LIKED THIS, YOU MIGHT ALSO ENJOY: RIDERS OF GLORY

A WESTERN HISTORICAL FICTION NOVEL BY ROBERT VAUGHAN

In the crucible of war, courage and conviction are forged like steel.

Colonel Nelson Pickett has spent his career carrying the scars of choices made and battles lost. Marked by the massacre at Wounded Knee and burdened by the weight of command, he believes a soldier's duty leaves no room for attachments. But as the Spanish-American War looms, his unwavering focus is tested by a spirited young journalist whose courage matches his own.

Marty McGuire is determined to prove herself in a world ruled by men. When she embeds with Pickett's Lightning Cavalry, she becomes an eyewitness to history—and a challenge to the hardened officer's rigid beliefs. As the horrors of war unfold, Nelson must face battles both on and off the field: the ruthless enemy ahead and the feelings he's tried to bury deep within.

When Marty is captured behind enemy lines, Nelson is forced to confront the cost of his decisions and the meaning of honor. In a world where survival demands sacrifice, can he reconcile duty with the stirrings of his heart?

AVAILABLE NOW

ABOUT THE AUTHORS

Robert Vaughan sold his first book when he was 19. That was 57 years and nearly 500 books ago. He wrote the novelization for the mini series Andersonville. Vaughan wrote, produced, and appeared in the History Channel documentary Vietnam Homecoming.

His books have hit the NYT bestseller list seven times. He has won the Spur Award, the PORGIE Award (Best Paperback Original), the Western Fictioneers Lifetime Achievement Award, received the Readwest President's Award for Excellence in Western Fiction, is a member of the American Writers Hall of Fame and is a Pulitzer Prize nominee.

Vaughn is also a retired army officer, helicopter pilot with three tours in Vietnam. And received the Distinguished Flying Cross, the Purple Heart, The Bronze Star with three oak leaf clusters, the Air Medal for valor with 35 oak leaf clusters, the Army Commendation Medal, the Meritorious Service Medal, and the Vietnamese Cross of Gallantry.

———

Chris Mullen is an accomplished and award-winning author, recognized for his captivating storytelling and literary talent. Hailing from Richmond, Texas, he is a proud graduate of Texas A&M University.

With a career spanning twenty-three years in education, Chris has been a dedicated teacher in both Kindergarten and PreK, cultivating his passion for storytelling and nurturing young minds. In 2019, he received the prestigious Connie Wootton Excellence in Teaching Award—a testament to his commitment to education and his profound impact on students' lives, bestowed upon him by the Southwest Association of Episcopal Schools (SAES). It was during this time that the idea for his young adult western adventure series, Rowdy, was born.

When he's not weaving stories, you can find Chris honing his craft in local coffee shops, pizza places, or even the neighborhood grocery store.

www.chrismullenwrites.com